AMANDINE

Also by Adele Griffin

Rainy Season
Split Just Right
Sons of Liberty
The Other Shepards
Dive
Witch Twins

AMANDINE

ADELE
GRIFFIN

DISCARD

HYPERION

New York

74494

For Donna Bray

With many thanks to Shannon Dean

Text copyright © 2001 by Adele Griffin

First Edition

3 5 7 9 10 8 6 4 2

Designed by Christine Kettner

Printed in the United States of America

Library of Congress Cataloging-in-Publication Data

Griffin, Adele.

Amandine / Adele Griffin.

p. cm.

Summary: Her first week at a new school, shy, plain Delia befriends
Amandine, not anticipating the dangerous turns their friendship would take.

ISBN 0-7868-0618-4 (trade) — ISBN 0-7868-2530-8 (library)

[1. Emotional problems—Fiction. 2. Schools—Fiction.

3. Massachusetts—Fiction.] I. Title.

PZ7.G881325 Am 2001

[Fic]—dc21

00-54010

Visit www.hyperionteens.com

PART ONE

I met Amandine on the last day of my first week at James DeWolf High School. She was standing on the curb outside the front doors, waiting to be picked up, and so was I. She wore an oversized white coat, the kind used by scientists, and her pale head was bowed as she stared down at her scuffed pink ballet slippers. The slump of her shoulders suggested she had been standing there for a long time.

The afternoon was cold; a March chill

furred with frost. Not a lab-coat-and-ballet-slippers kind of day. I myself was wearing thick brown wool things.

I did not think she could tell I was staring at her, but she knew. It was something I learned about her, later. That Amandine was always aware of her audience.

"In there," she began, in a voice that stayed smooth as a zipper. "I've got a notebook. Drawings of the ugliest things I ever saw in my entire life." She kicked her book bag, which crouched like a puppy at her feet. "Do you want to take a look?"

She turned her head to stare at me. Her eyes were hard and pebble gray.

I nodded yes.

"Five dollars," she said.

"I don't have any money on me," I lied.

"Sucks to be you."

A car pulled up. It was not like the sensible station wagons and minivans that the other mothers drove. This car was red and low, and when Amandine opened the door, music streamed out like an invitation to a private party. As she climbed inside I heard a man's voice say, in a way that was half joking and half not, "Dammit, Amandine, have the decency to *ask* before you go rip clothes from my closet."

That's how I learned her name. Amandine. At the time, that word sounded very beautiful.

"Did you meet anyone interesting today, Delia?" my mother asked me that evening. She is from Boston and enjoys polite conversation, even among family.

I saw the pull in her eyes as she waited, and my own eyes fixed on the Diet Delite carrot cake she had placed in view to get me through my tuna and broccoli. Mom did not eat with me, preferring to wait for Dad, who usually worked late now that he was working for himself. Then they would share their usual romantic dinner together in the dining room, after the Diet Delite cartons and I had been cleared out of sight.

Mom had asked me the same thing every evening since Monday, and every evening I had answered no. Tonight I answered, "Amandine."

"Well! Amandine who?"

"I don't know. Just Amandine."

"And what makes her so interesting, this Amandine?"

Using my index finger, I drilled a hole into my carrot cake. I wasn't hungry; Mrs. Gogglio had detoured through a drive-in Taco Bell before she dropped me off at home, and I had spent my money on three bean burritos plus curly fries.

My mother hated it when I played with my food, and I bet she was torn between waiting for an answer and wanting to scold me for my cake tunnel.

"*Dee*-lee-a . . . ?" she prompted, sing-song, a compromise.

"She likes to draw things," I answered. "She's an artist."

Amandine's name didn't come up again until the next morning. I was helping my parents turn up soil in the garden. The frost had turned to drizzle, but gardening was part of their optimistic list of "Things You Can Do in the Country That You Can't Do in the City." The City is New York. Every other city keeps its name, even Boston, which is a three-hour drive from us now.

It's been ten years since my parents left the City, and they still miss it enough to talk about all the ways it was a horrible place.

I am at the top of my parents' list of "Reasons We Left the City."

"You shouldn't keep a four-year-old there, in the City. It's wrong, like caging a bear," Mom used to say.

We've moved away from the City in increments over the years. First a hop upstate, then a jump over to Connecticut. Our latest leap, up here to Alford, puts us farther away from the City than we've ever been before.

It's quiet here. Lots of trees, and not many houses or people. I don't know why my parents are so nostalgic for skyscrapers and pigeons. I guess I'm more like my mom's brother, Uncle Steve, who says barefoot in green grass is as close to paradise as we mortals get.

"So, Honeydew, how would you rate your first week of school?" Dad asked. "I want details."

"Delia made a friend," Mom said. "Amandine. She's an artist."

"An artist? That right?" Dad looked expectant. "What else?"

Suddenly I had a feeling that she'd already filled him in on Amandine, and that they were playacting this conversation.

"Oh. Well, okay. She's got long hair." I struggled. "And she, um . . . takes ballet."

"Sophisticated lady." Dad smirked. It was his signature smirk, the one he'd used in his high school yearbook photo, back when he used to be handsome. The yearbook is on my bookshelf now; I've looked through it a thousand times plus. Dad's name then was "O"—short for "The Operator"—and all his yearbook messages make him sound lawless, stuff like: *"O, boy!—Little Egg Harbor, don't burn down the house!"* Or, from girls, in shy bubble script: *"U better not 4get me, O! love, Chrissy!"*

I've never seen Mom's yearbook, but probably she was popular, too, in her own proper-Bostonish, club-president-y way. Popular is all over her, in her smile, her pedicures, the way she knows the exactly perfect thing to say to a stranger. Once at a party I overheard her say that she was the nice girl who married the bad boy. She had giggled when she said it, which was why it stuck in my mind. My mother is not a giggler by nature.

"You should invite Amandine over to the house next weekend," Dad continued. "I give you my word it'll be in better shape. I'm putting up your curtains just as soon as I get around to it."

"Mmm," I answered.

"Ooh, that'd be fun," Mom put in. "A sleepover. I'd take off work early and drive you and Amandine to the movies or the mall, if you'd like. And," she coaxed, "you can get takeout for dinner, anything you want. Anything."

"Mmm."

"Delia, really," Mom added in a deeper, more meaningful tone. "It'd be good to make an effort. We know it's tough to move and transfer schools midyear, but Dad and I feel awful enough without you insisting on playing the loner."

"Playing the loner" was the phrase Mom used to explain away why I never had many friends. Her rationale was that I did it on purpose. There was no point in arguing; I think the idea was a comfort to her.

Mostly I know I'm lucky to be an only child, and I don't have to suffer being compared to some wonderful sister or brother. The one who "got everything"—Mom's hazel eyes and long lashes and Dad's curly hair, instead of the puddle-eyed, lank-haired combination that made me. But times like now I wish I had a brother. A cool, older brother named Ethan whose good looks and herds of friends fulfilled all of my parents' expectations, and took the pressure off me.

"I'll invite her over next weekend," I said on impulse. It got the right reaction. Mom made a soft approving noise in her throat. Dad's face brightened.

"Super. I'll make my famous sour-cherry pancakes." He smiled and rubbed his hands together.

My brain worked on it. Amandine, at my table. Ballet slippers kicking under the chair. Triangle kitten face and flat gray eyes taking in our big bright maplewood kitchen.

Sure, I'll have another pancake, Mr. Blaine!

Well, this wasn't a terrible picture.

The drizzle had turned to a spitting rain.

"We ought to go in," said Mom, collecting up her gardening tools. "Smell that! Soon we'll have daffodils and hyacinths. What a gorgeous spring this will be. You'd never get this kind of spring in the City!"

"Black lung, that's what the City'd have given me by now." Dad looked up at the sky and inhaled deeply as he hooked his fingers in his belt band to hoist up his jeans. Now that he's in business for himself, he'd taken to using his old neckties in place of belts. A regular belt would have done the job better, but he probably enjoyed the clownish look of the tie, of making a small joke on the corporate world he'd been happy to leave behind.

Amandine slipped the drawing into my locker early Monday morning. She meant to shock me and did, like a poke in the eye. I tried to make sense of what basically was a dirty picture of a twisted-up, burnt-up naked lady. Her hands and feet were charred, and she was color-markered in smeared, scalded-lasagna hues of yellow, black, and red.

Ugly as it was, Amandine had drawn it well. She was seriously talented.

Before I could think it through, my fingers crunched the picture into a ball. I crept down the crowded corridor in a fog of panic, furtive as a thief until I found the custodian's wheeled garbage cart, where I dropped it. Then I went to the girls' room and washed my tingling hand. It was as if that lady's actual scorched skin had touched mine.

Worse, the image in my head—that one of the pale, pretty girl eating sour-cherry pancakes in my kitchen—went up in smoke. Over the weekend, I had turned that girl, Amandine, into a daydream of friendship and secrets.

But the real Amandine was messed up, crazy. Bad.

Afterward, when mess lay thick and everywhere and everyone was blaming everyone else and some people were trying to lift the blame off me and other people were pressing it back on, I tried to remember my innocence. I tried to make myself believe that I hadn't known. That Amandine had tricked me, just like she fooled everyone else.

But I'd always known something was wrong with her. I'd known from that first picture.

I knew, but I was distracted. It was my second Monday at James DeWolf, and mostly I was just trying to get by. This week was different from last, when the luster of "new girl" had clung to me shiny as a wet lollipop. Last week, it seemed that everyone in the entire ninth grade had introduced him- or herself to me or saved me a seat or passed me a note or confided which teachers were insane or clueless or scared easy. Now, kids had figured out that I was nothing special. Nothing better than what I had been back in Connecticut.

Amandine didn't find me until after lunch. "Did you get my lady?" she asked, slipping up behind me as I was clearing the dirty silverware off my tray. She was more than a head shorter than I. Her breath seemed to stick to the hairs on my neck.

I shrugged and stepped away from her.

She stepped closer so that now she stood at my side. "What'd you think?"

"I threw her in the trash." My heart was kicking, knowing she'd be angry. I tried to stare her squarely down, but I'm no good at that kind of thing. I could feel myself smiling although I didn't mean it. My voice was watery, apologizing. "Sor-ry. Too gross."

"You cow!" she burst out. Then quickly, she recovered, smiled, showing me her pointy kitten teeth. She looked different when she smiled. A small twist that turned her charming. "You goof! *Gross* was the whole point! But if you threw mine away, you have to draw me something in replacement, right? Right?"

Another thing I would learn about Amandine. Everything, everything was either a bet or a bargain.

"I don't . . . I don't know." I swallowed.

"The Ugliest Thing you ever saw. You draw it for me. You have to."

"Yours was a lie, though. You never saw that lady."

"Yuh-huh, I did."

"In a movie?"

"In my brain."

"That doesn't count," I said. "Last week, you told me . . . you said you had to see it. That you had to see it for real."

"She was for real."

"Like in *life*, though."

"I never said that."

I was confused. What had she said, exactly? The lunch bell rang, startling us both, reminding me that we were not the only two people in the entire cafeteria.

* * *

Amandine cornered me after school. Since we were in different homerooms, and because I was in advanced math and English classes (my old school had been harder), lunch and spring fitness were our only shared periods, and we did not have spring fitness on Mondays.

She was lingering beside my locker. I knew she'd be there. I'd been jangly all afternoon, and my mouth tasted bitter from all the strange things I'd been chewing on, erasers and my hair and fingernails and the button on my shirt cuff.

"Your mom's always late, same as my dad," she said, speaking in that same smooth voice from last Friday. I was beginning to realize Amandine had different voices and used them as she saw fit. This one sounded as if she were in a play. "Let's go to the art room. Make *them* wait on *us* for a change.

Remember, you owe me, for what you did."

"That's not my mom; it's our neighbor, Mrs. Gogglio, and she'd be mad," I said. "It's one thing if it's the grown-up who's late. But if *I'm* not on time . . ." Amandine was already tugging on my arm. She didn't need to tug too hard. I followed, jittery with disobedience.

The art room was empty.

"It feels weird to be here without a teacher," I whispered. "Don't you think?"

She didn't answer. Instead, she stood on fragile slippered tiptoes and opened a cupboard. She pulled out a slice of pulpy construction paper and slid it onto one of the tables.

"My parents are artists. I'm an artist, too. And a ballet dancer, and an actress," she said, pirouetting to the shelves where the pencils and paints were kept. She grabbed a bundle of loose colored pencils from a box. "What about your parents?"

"My dad used to work for a bank. Now he's a freelance financial consultant," I said. "But my mother is an architect. She just joined Shelton-McCook. That's the best firm in Massachusetts." I was proud of Mom's job. It sounded glamorous, though she specialized in organizing spaces that were sort of boring, like parking lots and lobbies.

"Which one of them is fat?" asked Amandine.

"Neither of them," I said. Then I added, "But I'm not fat. I'm *overweight*."

"Oh, what a coincidence. I'm *under-height*," she answered. She laughed at her own joke, and after a minute, my own laugh joined hers, catching me by surprise. It was a relieved kind of laughing, like a splash of cold water on my face. Because being *over-*

weight was not funny, it had never been funny. *Overweight* was a problem that meant Diet Delite and trips to the doctor and my parents' pinched faces whenever they caught me with a cookie or a cheeseburger. *Overweight* was the thing about myself I hated most, the problem that had plagued me since before kindergarten.

But now, suddenly, today, it was funny.

We stood there laughing, and it was summer vacation for a minute, warm and free and just the two of us splashing around together in this cold water of happy laughing, right there in the empty art room of James DeWolf High School.

I drew Amandine a picture of a dead bird, a sparrow that had been zapped by an electric wire during last week's storm. Or that's what Dad had figured, but it also might have been plain, old-fashioned lightning. He had used a dustpan and newspaper to remove it from our backyard, but not before I'd got a good look at it, a body bag of feathers and bones so still and lumpy that it was hard to imagine it ever had soared on the breath of a breeze.

When I was finished, Amandine nodded her head in approval. "Now sign your name at the bottom," she instructed. "Like a witness."

Every evening after their supper, my father prepared chamomile tea for himself and my mother. He arranged it on a tray, pleating the napkins and fixing the butter cookies into a smile shape, as if he were delivering hotel room service. Midway through their tea was when I usually came in to kiss them good night.

That evening, standing in the doorway, it struck me that the den here in Alford looked exactly like the den back in Connecticut.

The glass-topped table was centered on the woven rug. The pillows were tipped just so in the window seat. The carved wooden ducks stared from the same height on the bookshelf. My parents were banked in the same positions on the couch, their legs crossed toward each other. And, as always, there were a few cookies left on the plate.

"Original use of space," I commented. It was sort of a family joke, since this was one of Mom's architect-y phrases she used when there was nothing else to say.

My father laughed. "Ah, but zee proof is in zee details, Inspector." He spoke in some kind of accent—it was probably a line from a movie; and I laughed along as if I knew which one.

Lexi Neumann, my best friend back in Connecticut, used to say that if my dad was our age, he'd never want to hang out with us. "Face it," she told me. "He's Prince

Charming, and we're more like court jesters." She was right, it was true. Is true. My father's charm is powerful. Turned on, the spotlight of his attention warms you from head to feet. Switched off, he can make you feel about as appealing as a pair of old sneakers, as if the only reason you're around was because there was no place else to toss you. Last week, when I got my physical and my mother reported that Dr. Hurtebeise had suggested I trim down a little, Dad had folded his arms and regarded me with the old-sneakers face.

"How hard could it be?" he'd asked. "You have to learn to live with a little hunger. How hard could it be, Delia?"

I didn't know the answer.

Tonight, having made the right joke and laughed at his accent, I stood in the full wattage of his spotlight. His smile made me glow, made me warm, and I knew that to take a cookie off the plate was to risk the lights-out, a return of the old-sneakers stare.

I could live with a little hunger. Of course I could.

Tuesday, Amandine had saved a place for me in the cafeteria.

"Delia!" she called, waving me over.

I felt purposeful and happy as I pushed through the crowd to sit with her. All the previous week, I had been eating lunches with Samantha Blitz, who had been assigned to show me around, and whose patience I was testing. Samantha was the starting center on the freshman girls' soccer team, and at lunch she always sat with her teammates, who had been perfectly nice and had become perfectly indifferent.

"Hi." I slid my tray opposite hers and sat.

"Do you smell anything?" She leaned forward.

I sniffed. The air was fruity, spiced with bread and bananas and tacos, the hot lunch special of the day.

"What should I smell?"

"I forgot to put on deodorant this morning. I can't believe I would ever forget a thing like that, I've been doing it for so long. I have to shave practically twice a day, too. I'm very developed, that way."

I didn't say anything, though what she had said was tough to believe. Amandine was small and pale and boyish, and she looked younger than fourteen. As if she knew what I was thinking, she reached behind into her backpack and pulled out a black glasses case, snapped it open, then slipped on a pair of hexagonal wire-rimmed glasses.

"Nonprescription," she informed me. "Don't they make me look older?" She tilted her head from one side to another, modeling.

It seemed important for her that I answer yes, so I did.

"You watch," she said, running a speculative finger over the frame. "This shape'll be, like, a total trend by next week. Kids always copy me, I don't know why. DeWolf's got a lot of followers. Were kids here the same as in your old school? A sheep herd?"

"Maybe. But kids here seem nicer." I shrugged. "Alford has a softer aesthetic." I didn't know what aesthetic meant, exactly, but I'd heard my mother say that to someone on the phone. "That's why we moved. It's a good place for my dad to start his own business and be his own boss, blah blah blah." I shrugged, as if my parents' spontaneity made no difference to me. In truth, our move to Alford, which they had not consulted me on, had come as an unsettling surprise. But my parents always worked as a unit, whereas I was more like the overpacked luggage they carted along with them.

Amandine grinned and rolled her eyes. "My parents did that, too. We used to live in New York City, actually. Brooklyn Heights, till I was in sixth grade. Then all of a sudden they wanted to hug trees and mow the lawn and stuff."

"Same as mine!"

"But they should go back. 'Cause of missing the plays and museums. They're both really, really into the arts."

"Same as mine!" Which was not quite true, but it wasn't as if my parents were *against* the arts. And suddenly, Amandine was at my breakfast table again, eating sour-cherry pancakes, talking to Mom about Times Square and Central Park.

As the ending lunch bell rang, I saw Samantha Blitz leave her table and walk over to us.

"Either of you guys seen my lucky bandanna?" she asked. "I lost it."

"That makes it an *un*lucky bandanna." Amandine smirked.

"What color is it?" I asked.

"It's goldish-orange, flower-y," she answered. "I was wearing it in homeroom."

"Oh, yes. I remember," I said, nodding. "Definitely, I'll keep an eye out. Gold and orange. Flowers. Got it. I'll keep a look out." I could hear myself sound overeager. Mom would have handled this better, with her Boston blend of friendly and indifferent.

Amandine yawned and stretched her arms over her head and said nothing.

"Okay. Well, yeah. If you happen to." Samantha's eyes skimmed over me and held Amandine's a second too long. "Later, guys."

"Me and her used to hang out a lot together," Amandine confided after

Samantha had left. She smiled kittenishly. "But that was before I found you."

Yesterday, after I'd kept her waiting, Mrs. Gogglio had given me some heat.

"Don't fritter away my goodwill, Delilah," she said. She had a hard time with my name, calling me Dahlia and Delayla before settling on this one. I'd corrected her for a little while, and then stopped bothering.

"Sorry, Mrs. Gogglio."

"It's not about the money, why I pick you up. It's about *coincidence*. I get off my shift at Sunrise Assisted at three and you get off school at three ten and our living right 'round the corner from each other makes this meeting a *coincidence*. But you'd be looping back roads on that school bus for an hour and then some if it wasn't for me. And I wouldn't have a heart to care, except it's on my way, and why not earn a little extra on the side? But my main point here is *coincidence*, you hear?"

"I'm sorry, Mrs. Gogglio. Really." It was hard to follow her every word, the way she said *hot* for heart and *un* for earn. She was Massachusetts *bohn* and raised, she'd told us proudly that first day she stopped over for a neighborly visit, bringing us a batch of blueberry muffins so good I couldn't seem to stop reaching for the next.

"Enjoy your starch, I see," she'd said, nodding me up and down as I bit into a third. *Stahch*, the word in Mrs. Gogglio's mouth meant all delicious things. She liked her starch, too, unlike my starch-free parents. Block-shouldered, apple-faced Mrs. Gogglio could have been my real, long-lost mother. And so our friendship was born. It wasn't completely about coincidence. After a day spent tending to old people, Mrs.

Gogglio seemed to enjoy the change of more youthful company. And after my own day of trying not to do or say the wrong thing or have the wrong answer or sit in the wrong place, Mrs. Gogglio's easy manner was a relaxing tonic.

Yesterday, as punishment for my lateness, Mrs. Gogglio didn't stop for a drive-through snack.

Today, I was right on time, as Amandine had left early on account of a doctor's appointment. It was Mrs. Gogglio who was about fifteen minutes late. She gave me her version of an apology as I got into her car.

"You hungry?"

"Not really. I don't know."

"Delilah, you look like the cat that swallowed the canary," she remarked as we turned onto the highway. "You're settling in good over there at the new school?"

"Sort of . . . with this one girl."

"That so?"

"Yep. She's kind of different from anyone I ever knew back in Connecticut. But she's nice."

"Nice means a lot."

"Yep." Though now *nice* seemed like the exactly wrong word to describe Amandine.

"Melissa MacKnight?" she asked hopefully. Melissa MacKnight was Odie MacKnight's granddaughter, and Odie was one of Mrs. Gogglio's favorite patients at Sunrise Assisted. But Melissa MacKnight had all the friends she needed.

"No. Her name's Amandine. Amandine Elroy-Bell."

"Elroy-Bell. Bell, Bell. Don't ring one." Mrs. Gogglio snorted. "Lived here long, those Elroy-Bells? I thought I'd heard most names 'round Alford."

"On State Road. In a big stone mansion, is how Amandine described it. Right on the corner, it's got an iron gate wrapped around it."

Mrs. Gogglio's face knit. "Ah. *Those* folks," she said after a pause. Out of the corner of my eye, I watched her face go blank as her thoughts turned private. I waited, nervous with curiosity. Mrs. Gogglio would have the right opinion. Her white Sunrise Assisted nursing uniform made her seem authoritative and reliable.

Whatever she was thinking, though, she kept it to herself.

"How about let's stop off at Friendly's?" she suggested presently. "Fries and Fribbles. Salty and sweet. I've got a two-for-one coupon for it in my book in the glove box. It'll be my treat."

"I don't know," I said. "I'm trying to lose . . . my mother wants . . ."

"Delilah," she said impatiently, "your skinny-miss mother's got no business trying to alter how you're built. There's no shame in a natural, healthy appetite." Her cheeks blazed with a pink fire of emotion. "Fact is, she should be proud of your nice strong looks."

Of course, her little speech didn't make sense; but when Mrs. Gogglio talked like that, I could actually feel myself settle better into the fit of my skin.

It would be another week before I met "*those folks,*" and saw that big house on State Road for myself. But my parents were pressing too hard for this weekend, wanting proof of Amandine. It was a relief when she agreed to stay over at my house Friday night, exactly one week after we had met.

"My mom's taking off early from work," I told her when I finally caught up with her on Friday afternoon after school. "She's picking us up out front and driving us to the mall and stuff. If we want movies and pizza."

"Pizza." Amandine rolled her eyes. "Pizza gives me zits."

"It doesn't have to be pizza. Where's your bag?"

"In my locker, where else?"

"Let's go get it."

She yawned an answer. She had been making me uneasy all day. First showing up for school that morning in a full, black-and-white striped skirt, large gold hoop earrings, and red lipstick. Then ignoring me, not seeking me out at my locker, and being so late to lunch that I had to eat through most of it in excruciating aloneness.

When I finally caught up to her, she acted indifferent. She had been enjoying the attention of her outfit all day, and the spotlight gave Amandine a strange radiance.

"Oh, dress it up, Amandine!" I heard

some girls laugh as we walked together down the hall. "Look at that skirt! Woweee!"

"It's my Natalie Wood from *West Side Story* costume," she told me offhandedly. "I'd let you borrow it, but we're different sizes."

"Oh, well." I made a show of looking disappointed, although I couldn't imagine risking the whispers and stares that would follow such a weird costume.

The day before in silent study period, I had overheard girls talking more meanly about Amandine, about her stop-sign-shaped glasses and the green opera gloves she had worn to school last week in place of winter gloves. But nobody was so bold to her face. To her face, Amandine was dealt with light teasing or quiet suspicion. Nothing worse. At my old school, treatment might have been different. I wouldn't have called them a sheep herd, exactly, but the kids here were pretty mild.

As we walked to her locker, she rubbed off most of the lipstick with the back of her hand and pulled up her hair. By the time Mom drove up to collect us, Amandine had transformed herself into a less Hollywood-style, more typical fifties-style girl, her ponytail and puffy skirt swinging as she walked to the car.

"Hi, Mrs. Blaine!" she sang, bubbly and sweet as an ice-cream soda. "I'm Amandine Elroy-Bell. Thanks for letting Delia invite me over to your home for the weekend!"

My mother looked positively joyful. "Why, it's my pleasure. You know, Delia's been talking about you all week!"

"Has she? What does she say?" Amandine played out a reaction of joy, then helped herself to the front seat without asking. I took the back, not sure whether to be mortified at Mom's comment, annoyed at Amandine's nerve, or relieved that neither of them needed me to be the conversation mediator.

It was obvious that Mom and Amandine would get along just fine.

"You're rich, huh?"

It was the first thing Amandine had said out of my mother's earshot. True to her plan, Mom had swung us through the mall for takeout and movie rentals, and only gave me one stern look when Amandine got a skinless chicken Caesar salad while I ordered an individual-sized pepperoni pizza at the takeout. But Mom had said I could have anything, and I could practically hear Mrs. Gogglio, all fired up, telling me that there was no shame in choosing what would sustain my nice strong shape.

After we got home, Mom, probably exhausted by Amandine's perky, phony questions ("What do you like best about living here, Mrs. Blaine? Have you been to the greenmarket yet? What kinds of flowers are you and Mr. Blaine going to plant?"), disappeared into the study to call work.

"Us? Rich? Not really," I answered. "We're just normal."

"It's okay. My parents are rich, too. Richer than yours, even, but they put a lot into savings. So it's not like I'm jealous. Show me your room?"

"Upstairs."

She followed me, sighing under the weight of her unwieldy bag. It seemed that she had packed a lot of stuff for a single night.

The upstairs was small and all mine, an eaves-sloped bedroom, a bathroom, and another, sealed-off storage space at the end of a short hall.

"Your bedroom is decorated very *bourgeois*," Amandine pronounced, dropping her bag as she entered it. "Do you know what that word means?"

I made a thoughtful face as if I might. "I like it anyway."

"Very matchy-match, that's what it means. You have lots of books, ugh. Books go too slow for my pace. If I have to read, it's for a play audition."

She seemed unimpressed by my room, which my parents and I had assembled in two days as soon as I'd confirmed that Amandine would be coming over. Prairie-flower curtains and dust ruffle, an oval rug, and a vase of store-bought flowers. Last night it had looked pretty; now it made me feel dumb and matchy-match.

"What's down the hall?" she asked.

"The bathroom."

"No, the other room."

"That? That's just my brother's room," I said. My words tumbled easy as a throw of the dice. "My older brother," I added.

"You didn't tell me you had a brother." Amandine regarded me with suspicion. "I thought you were like me. An only."

"I never said that."

"So where is he?"

"Oh. Where? He's in college," I said. It felt as if I was speaking through my nose.

"What's his name?"

"Ethan. He plays football. My parents really, really miss him, so if you didn't talk about him, at all I mean, that would be, um, better."

"Okay."

"And I'm not allowed to go in his room. It's locked, anyway." This part of my story was not a lie. Mom had put a hasp and buckle on the door on account of the exposed fiberglass insulation in the floor and walls. I don't know what exactly she thought I was going to do—sneak in and roll around in the fiberglass like a horse in clover? But my mother is protective that way. Ever since I could remember, she'd needed to straighten, order, lock, and guard things.

The sound of a car pulling into the driveway interrupted us.

"My dad," I said, gratefully.

Partly I lied to Amandine about Ethan because I wished it was true. I guess that's the reason most people lie. But I also lied because I had a feeling that I could get away with it, since Amandine herself was not very careful with the truth.

In fact, throughout that first week of our friendship, Amandine had been serving up some pretty questionable stories. They were always intriguing—like the one about her being chosen for the New York City Ballet Company's corps de ballet, but then getting shinsplints at the last minute. Or about dancing at a nightclub in Miami where Amandine was on the same dance floor as Madonna, and Madonna started copying her dance moves, and then everyone started copying Madonna, so she, Amandine, ended up not getting any credit for them. Or about how she had rescued a cat from the branch of a tree that was so high up and delicate that not even a fireman could get to it, but then the cat had scratched up Amandine's arm. Bloodied it so badly that she'd immortalized it in her notebook of Ugliest Things. She had shown me this drawing as "proof." She had used red nail polish for blood gashes, and the effect was pretty disgusting.

Fun to hear, but hard to imagine. And no matter what the setting, Amandine always flitted through it in the same role, as a nymph and a victim bruised by some minor cruelty. Which wasn't how the real Amandine was at all.

So what was one imaginary brother, tucked away in the setting of some far-off college? (I would make it Seattle or San Francisco, if she asked!) As soon as I'd dared it, though, the weight of my lie made me feel as if I had a raw egg balanced on my head. One misstep, and this dumb story would splatter. My parents would think I'd gone nuts, and worse, Amandine would know my lonely secret, something about me that seemed too private to have given her.

It was too late now.

"The much-anticipated Miss Amandine Elroy-Bell!" my father called up the stairs as soon as he walked in the door. "Reveal yourself!"

Amandine's eyes widened. She took out her cakey red lipstick and blotted it over her mouth. Then fluttered down the stairs, holding a pose midway, actress-style.

"*Mis*-ter Blaine, the pleasure is all mine!"

It was as if a TNT movie star had leaped off the screen and into our home. I clumped behind her at a distance. Dad's face couldn't hide his surprise, but since he was the one who had begun the silly movie talk, he sort of had to keep it going.

"What an utterly charming skirt!"

"This little old thing? Don't be silly. But you do know how to make a girl feel pretty, *Mis*-ter Blaine!"

Mom had entered the front hall. Her hand limply held her cell phone, her eyebrow quirked as she watched them.

"Hello, Daniel," she said.

"Hello, *Mis*-sus Blaine!" Dad copied Amandine's inflection while quickly turning away from her. He swung Mom into a big hug and a gobbling kiss that immediately embarrassed everyone, Dad included.

"The girls are having takeout, but I thought you and I . . ." Mom's voice lowered as she and he began their routine arm-in-arm stroll into the study for quiet time. I tugged at Amandine's wrist.

"Hey, let me show you out back, where we have a—"

She shook off my hand, hopped down a few steps. "Aren't we all eating together?" she called sharply after my parents. "As a family?"

My ears strained through the silence that followed. I washed it out with my own whisper. "Amandine, I don't usually . . . it wouldn't be as fun . . . with them."

"Is that what you'd like, Amandine?" My mother spoke up in her best Boston-hostess voice. Yet I could hear that she was annoyed.

"It's what I *thought*," Amandine answered in a cold, adult voice of her own. As if the power of what she assumed should be enough to change what had been planned.

* * *

Mom set dinner for four in the dining room. Silverware and linen napkins and bread rolls for everyone, takeout for us, and quail and creamed spinach for my parents. Amandine even dressed for it by donning a short black jacket, the kind that bullfighters wear. Plus more lipstick and dark rings of eyeliner that made her face look hungry.

I tried on some of her lipstick, pressing it deep into my lips, tasting its wax.

"You're not ready for that color," she said, laughing when she saw. "You should stick to pink. How do I look?" She sucked in her cheeks and arched her neck.

"Fine, I guess. Who cares?"

She laughed again and brushed past me, heading down the stairs.

I followed. I was nervous of my freshly leaked lie. I chewed my tongue and hoped nobody would ask the wrong questions, and

I silently practiced my defensive answers, if it came to that.

"I brought *Carmen*," Amandine announced to my parents as soon as we sat down. "With Teresa Berganza, on DVD. Shall I put it on? Do you have a DVD player? Do you even like opera?" The last question was a bit wistful.

"Why, yes, that would be just . . . perfect, Amandine." My mother looked surprised, then pleased. "It's in the living room, dear. In that silver-and-wood-paneled cabinet. You'll have to raise the volume so that we can hear it in here."

Amandine nodded. As her jacket fell open, I saw that she had brought the discs down with her, slipped into an inside pocket. I also saw that at some point she had changed from her black blouse to a sexy, plunge-necked black leotard. Although there was nothing much to see, the leotard humiliated me as much as if I were wearing it, instead.

She skipped out of the room, and I glanced at my parents to see if they were shocked, exasperated, anything, but they were speaking quietly to each other.

"*Carmen*," Mom mused to Dad. "I've always preferred it to *Romeo and Juliet*."

"I haven't heard it in ages."

"Oh, let's light the candles!" Amandine exclaimed when she returned.

Dad jumped out of his seat for his Brookstone electric lighter kept in the sideboard drawer. Then he dimmed the lights and lit both candelabras.

"Ah, that's wonderful! I forget what candlelight does to a room." Mom clasped her hands together and held them under her chin.

It did look pretty. The icy March twilight outside; the warm, golden firelight inside; and all of us gathered together while

Carmen washed in at a soothing distance. A family, Amandine had said. And it made me sort of angry, though I couldn't have said exactly why.

"This is the first time I ever ate in here," I blurted.

"Stands to reason. We've been here less than a month," said Dad. "And Miss Amandine is our first special occasion." He smirked across the table at Amandine, giving her his lawless Operator's smirk. As if he were teasing her and complimenting her at the same time.

"Who, little old me?" she asked, pointing a finger at herself.

I wished she would stop with all that. The way she talked to my dad was worse than the way she talked to my mom. Fussy and chirpy was one thing, but flirty was another. She should know better than to talk to other people's dads this way. It was alarming.

My parents were unalarmed. They drank up Amandine as if she were an entertainment or an amusement, like the special red wine they treated themselves to in the summer. Even when, at one point, Amandine put down her fork and began to sing along with the opera—which made me shiver slightly, it was too weird—they did not react except to smile and listen, their heads tilted like birds.

I could almost hear Dad say, "Young and refreshing! Just bold enough!"

After dinner, we parted—Amandine and I to the living room to watch movies, and my parents to clean up the kitchen.

Later, while I was fixing a tray of fruit and cookies in the pantry, Mom caught me around my shoulders and drew me into a clumsy hug. "Such fun!" she whispered in my ear. "She's a water sprite, your little friend."

"Kind of unpredictable," I said. Though

I didn't quite know if I was referring to Amandine or my mother's reaction to her.

We both slept in my bed, on opposite sides. I wasn't used to sharing my bed, it made me nervous, and when my toe accidentally touched Amandine's leg, she judo-kicked me.

"Sorry," I said, although it was all her fault.

"Good night," she answered stiffly. I supposed she didn't want to share the bed any more than I did. I wished she had brought a sleeping bag. A sleeping bag was kind of the rule of a sleepover, and I didn't get how Amandine could have forgotten this.

"Your parents wouldn't like it if I broke in and slept in your brother's room, huh?" she hissed after a few more shifting, twisting minutes.

I felt my heart stumble. "They would kill me," I answered. "I'm not kidding."

"There's no pictures of him anywhere. Are they mad at him?"

"Oh, yes!" I answered. "They're so mad. Because. Because he wanted to marry this girl, and they didn't like her, so he's not talking to them. Ethan's really good-looking and tons of girls are in love with him, so my parents have these really high standards. You don't see it, but they can be very strict if they want."

"They love him the most," she whispered. "That's why they're mad."

"I don't know about that." And for a moment, I felt a throb of pity for myself, and more than a little jealousy of this wonderful, made-up brother of mine.

I woke up several times that night, and each time I sensed that Amandine was awake, too. It made my dreams skittish, and

I was conscious all night that the bottoms of my feet were dry and scratchy. At one point toward morning, I was sure Amandine had slipped out of the bed and was no longer in my room, but by then I was too tired to care.

I woke late, and my opened eyes felt bruised. From downstairs, I heard Amandine's voice. I smelled coffee and pancakes. Nobody had bothered to call me. When I sat up, I saw the bath towel and pools of discarded clothes on the floor. I saw, too, that the books on my shelf, as well as my painted cigar box of treasures, my bronze horseshoe bookends, and my chorus line of old Beanie Babies were askew, as if everything had been taken out, examined, and hastily replaced.

I leaped out of bed to check on everything, to make sure all of my treasures were there. My fingers counting, reassuring me that nothing was gone.

Nothing was gone. But still! How sneaky! What was she looking to steal? My heart pounded so loud that I thought I could feel its reverberation in the floorboards.

Furious, knotting my robe, I stormed down the stairs and into the kitchen.

"Honeydew!" said Dad. He and Mom and Amandine were ringed around their empty plates on the breakfast table. My parents' faces were alive with pleasure.

"Honeydew!" Amandine grinned. Her wire-rimmed glasses were perched on the edge of her nose, giving her a smart, thoughtful appearance. I felt sleepy and childish in contrast.

"Amandine was just telling us that she was in the City last month, to see that revival of *Watch on the Rhine*," said Mom. "It's a play." She turned to Amandine and spoke confidentially. "Poor Delia doesn't have good parents who have been as conscientious about her cultural awareness."

And Dad laughed in a sporty, ho-ho way that I had never heard before.

I moved to the overhead cabinet for a plate.

"Delia, I thought you might like some fruit and yogurt," said Mom. "It's already prepared, in a glass dish in the fridge."

I veered away from the cabinet as gracefully as I could, opened the refrigerator, and took my breakfast to my place.

"As I was saying," Dad continued, "back when we lived in the City, Eva and I used to go to the Sunday matinee special. You could get a fixed-price lunch at that restaurant, what was it called . . . the trattoria on Thirty-eighth with the free homemade grappa, lord help me, what was the name of that place, Eva?"

"La Bugga? No, that's not . . . La Trugga?" Mom rippled her fingers over her forehead as she tried to remember.

"La Gubbria?" suggested Amandine.

"La Gubbria!" Mom and Dad exclaimed together, then burst out laughing.

Watching the three of them, I felt all mixed-up and confused. It was as if a bubble had sealed them off from me. Now I was the guest, the outsider, and Amandine was the daughter. A strange gypsy daughter who looked more mature than usual, dressed as she was in a Hanes V-neck, jeans, and clogs, and I wondered why that costume had won out over the other choices.

It was starting to upset me, all of it. That Amandine had snooped in my room, that she was allowed to eat pancakes, that she knew the name of the stupid restaurant with the free grappa. I ate my yogurt and fruit in silence, and stayed quiet as I helped with the cleanup, waiting for my parents to head out to the garden before I confronted her. She was pirouetting around the floor, glasses in hand and a dishrag on her head.

"My mantilla," she said.

"Amandine, did you go through the stuff on my bookshelf?"

"What are you talking about?"

"Because that's personal, okay? If you went through it, I'll . . . I'll never speak to you again."

She stopped, looking stricken even as she continued to hold her ballet pose. "God, I'm sorry, Delia. Maybe that was bad of me, but you don't have to be horrible. All I did was look at your Horse Club books. Oh, and then I took out your dad's yearbook. It was right there, and I wanted to see for myself. How you said how he used to be real handsome. By the way, could I borrow *The Noplace Pony*?"

"What else did you do? Did you take anything?"

"Nothing." She held up her hands, palms flat.

"Promise."

"Promise! Double-cross my heart. I'm sorry."

But I had a feeling that neither the promise nor the apology meant much to her.

"Watch me do ballet?" she asked. "I'm playing *Coppelia*. Do you recognize it?"

She began to hop and spring around. I watched. She was a trained dancer—that was no lie—so her spins and leaps were strong and precise. She twirled out to the living room and turned the music up so loud that eventually my parents drifted in.

"Live from Blaine Center," Dad joked.

"Shhh." Mom put a hand on his arm. She watched, riveted. The skinny daughter she wished she had. The daughter who "got everything."

With an audience, Amandine went

faster, performed better. I sensed my parents' enchantment, and I longed for secret abilities of my own, to be something better than what they could see. The tiny ballerina inside my own dull self danced along with Amandine, shadowing every pretty step. Well, at least I had brought her to them. At least I had done something they appreciated.

At the end, she pliéd low, bowing as we applauded. I made my clapping slow, so that it sounded rude. But I'd had enough.

"When are your parents coming to get you?" I asked. "It's almost noon."

"Mom's not there. My dad called earlier, while you were sleeping, he's going to be late." Amandine bit her lip. "But I just realized, I have my doctor's appointment in town. Physical therapy, for my shinsplints. I forgot to tell him."

"Call home now and tell him," I said.

"He's in his studio. He won't hear the phone."

"I could give you a lift to town," offered Dad. "I was going to the hardware store. It's not really on the way, but if you want—"

"Great!"

He looked surprised, but smoothed over it quickly. "You want to come along, Delia? I won't be at the store for more than a few minutes."

"No, thanks," I said. "I've got homework." An ironclad excuse.

"Eva?"

"If I go, then I can't finish putting the fish fertilizer on the topsoil. I want to get the smell over and done with."

Dad nodded, but now he looked put out. Maybe the idea of enduring half an hour of Amandine and her constant showing off was giving him second thoughts. Bad luck. She was his problem now.

"Funny how what goes around comes around," said Mom, sliding up next to me at the door frame as I watched them leave, Amandine dragging her bag because Dad forgot to take it from her. "I used to wear clogs and jeans back when I was in grad school. I haven't seen a pair of clogs like that in almost twenty years. Our Amandine has a unique style."

"Just because she's wearing it doesn't mean it's any kind of style," I bit back. My words sounded small, but I didn't want her to be *our* Amandine. She could come for a visit, but any ownership of her seemed suffocating. Even the clogs seemed sneaky, as if she was trying to show how much she belonged to us.

When she didn't. She didn't.

Monday morning, Samantha Blitz was getting off the bus just as I was getting out of

Mrs. Gogglio's car. I had my chance and I leaped for it. My hand groped in my book bag for the bandanna.

"Samantha!" I called, running up to her and thrusting it into her hands. "Here! I found this last week. It was hanging over the shower rod in the girls' locker room. I know you have a game today and—"

"Oh my gosh! Delia, awesome!" She snatched it from my fingers and shook it out, flipped it over. "I figured it was just, you know, totally gone! You're the best!"

When a practically perfect girl like Samantha Blitz says you're the best, it really feels as if, for a moment, you are.

"I meant to give it back Friday, but you had soccer and I had spring fitness and we were in the gym and you were all outside so I put it in my book bag, and then some other stuff was going on for the weekend and I totally forgot! I'm so stupid!"

I was talking too much, too fast. Then I saw the low red car, the one that dropped off Amandine, turn into the parking lot. I stalled an extra moment, looking at Samantha. Hoping. Samantha just smiled.

"Okay," she said. "Thanks, again."

"Okay. I better go," I said.

Later, when Samantha and her boyfriend, Marcus Zeller, passed me in the hall, she waved. A ripple and drop of the free hand that wasn't hooked around Marcus's belt loop. But it wrenched me. Samantha seemed so normal, like a bar of soap, after I'd spent a week soaked in oil. My oil was Amandine, and even when I was not with her, the marked territory of our friendship clung to me.

Now I knew Samantha Blitz was out of my reach. The bandanna had been my last lucky chance, and I hadn't figured out how to make it work.

Sitting with Amandine at lunch, I tried not to let my eyes stray to Samantha and her rowdy, happy table as I half listened to Amandine relate her plan to cut class. An afternoon assembly had been scheduled for freshmen and sophomores, some slide show from some teacher who went someplace and took some pictures there. It sounded boring, but I'd never been a class-cutter.

"Oh, come on." Amandine's gray eyes were contemptuous. "There's too many of us for Mrs. Nyeung and Ms. Hunnington to keep it all together. That's why they yell so much, 'cause they're going nuts. Look, you get in the end of the line, and when it turns the corner to go down to the theater, cut into the bathroom. Not the girls' but the teachers' one. I'll meet you there."

"What if a teacher comes in?"

"Then she'll send us back to the the-ater, or blue-slip us for Saturday study hall." She crossed her arms. "But the probability is almost zero, Delia. Don't disappoint me."

I tried to imagine getting a Saturday study hall. My parents would be furious. But Amandine seemed so sure that she made me feel a little daring. And if Amandine didn't attend the assembly, then who would I sit with in the theater? Samantha Blitz? That would be pushing my luck. No, I'd end up sitting alone near the teachers or, worse, in a spare seat in front of a row of jock guys— an hour's worth of chair kicks and spitballs aimed into my hair.

I cut. Keeping to the end of the line, then swaying, wobbling until I veered out of it completely. Anxiety put a rosy glow in my face that must have made me look guilty from miles away as I scurried into the teachers' bathroom.

Amandine was hiding in a stall. She

sprang out and slapped me a high five. We waited, breath held, until the din of the passing line faded. Then we made a break for it, Amandine ahead and I following sweatily behind. Down two flights on the fire escape stairs and into the soundproof sub-terrain of the music department.

She led me into a little room that was a storage space for the harp and the electric standup organ. A long row of greasy polyester blue choir outfits, separated by plastic dry cleaner's bags, hung from a wall-to-wall clothes rod. Other than that, the room was empty.

"What are we doing here?" I asked.

"Shhh!" She pinched my arm. I heard voices slowly approaching. The door was louvered, slicing up my view of what lay behind it.

"That's Mr. Serra out there," I yipped. Mr. Serra was the school principal.

"Oh, who cares?" Amandine shrugged, but we waited until the voices had passed. Then she said, "Let's do a skit."

"A what?"

"A skit. You pretend you're that maintenance guy who mows the grass, and I'll be me, and you ask me out on a date but I have a big black poppy seed stuck in my teeth and I don't know it, so you have to try to tell me!"

"That's weird," I said.

"No, it's *acting*," she answered. "It's for fun. I used to be in plays all the time. From, like, age three to age eleven I was always in a play at the Circle Theater, back when we lived in Brooklyn." She began to tick them off with her fingers. "*Inherit the Wind, Really Rosie, The Children's Hour, The Prime of Miss Jean Brodie*. Tons more. Come on, Delia. Do it with me."

"I don't know how to be a guy."

"Then I'll be him." She spun away into the corner of the room, her back to me. "I'm getting into character," she said over her shoulder. When she faced me again, she had her shoulders flexed and her face mirrored the casually alert expression of the man who for the past week had been taking care of the school grounds. He was older, but handsome in a sunburned, burnt-out way.

"Hey," Amandine the lawn-guy said in a low voice.

"Hi," I said uncertainly.

"You look good in that shirt."

"Thanks," I said. I smiled, unsure if I wanted to play this game. The gray eyes took in my smile, then narrowed in faint disgust. The black poppy seed! I clamped my mouth shut.

"Uh, so are you busy Thursday?" she asked, smirking. Her smirk reminded me of

Dad's Operator expression. It struck me that she was imitating it.

"Mmm." I put my hand over my mouth.

"What are you trying to hide? I bet you have a real pretty smile." She swaggered closer. "Why are you hiding that smile? I've been watching you a long time, girl. You're really mature-looking for your age." She scooched her face up into mine. Then tried to pry off my hand.

"Stop it! Stop it!" I twisted away, my stomach fluttering. It was hard not to feel that, in a peculiar way, Amandine really was the lawn guy. She was strangely convincing.

"Come on, Delia. It's Delia, isn't it?" Amandine the lawn guy persisted. "That's a really sexy name."

I couldn't hold it in any longer, and I started laughing.

"Uh, what's so funny?" Still being the guy, she rubbed the tip of her nose. "Hey, uh, Delia, I think you've got something stuck . . ." She bared her own teeth and tapped one. "Right between your two front . . ."

"Stop it! Stop it!" I bent double, hiding my face. My hysterical choking laughter finally made her break character and she started laughing, too. It was so stupid, there was no reason for it, but laughing was like a cold flood, a release, the same as that day in the art room. We laughed and couldn't stop; we stamped our feet and muffled the sounds of our voices by pushing our faces into the plastic-covered choir robes, although I'd heard you could suffocate yourself doing something like that.

PART TWO

We started performing skits all the time after that, usually at lunch or spring fitness or after school. It saved our friendship, I guess. Or maybe it was the friendship. The skits were weird, fun weird, and the fun was a private kind of fun. Amandine always set them up—she had a better imagination for them. The rules were that one person would act the part of herself and the other would be the character of someone unpredictable. Then Amandine would create a situation.

At first, I could only play myself. Amandine didn't seem to mind.

"You be you, and I'll be moron Mark Ingersell," she would start. (Mark was in our grade; he was gorgeous and failing all his classes.) "And we're lab partners, and you try to get me to go out on a date with you."

"You be you, and I'm Samantha Blitz and you have to ask me for a tampon."

"You be you, and I'm Mr. Serra and you have to tell me that my fly is undone."

Amandine was so good; her face could reflect the smallest tic—Samantha's open-mouthed listening, Mr. Serra's reflexive habit of clearing his throat, Mark Ingersell's slight stammer. Eventually, she could make me believe that part of her really was that person, and that's when she'd throw in the wrench.

"Honey," she would say, clearing her throat as Mr. Serra, "you can't go pointing to a principal's pants like that. Now I know I'm, *ahem*, a foxy guy. *Ahem*. So if you promise not to tell your parents, I think we could arrange a little, *ahem*." She'd start winking, coughing, leering, but by then I would be unstrung in laughing hysterics.

"There go the giggle girls," teachers would say as we snickered and whispered down the halls, deep into our skit right up until we had to pull apart at different doors. Sometimes I risked lateness, and Mrs. Gogglio's wrath, and we sneaked in a music room skit after school. The room was almost always deserted, but I never stopped being scared that we would be discovered. And then one day, we were.

We were doing a skit where I accidentally go into the boys' room. Amandine was pretending to be a strange, silent kid in our class named Dylan Humes. Amandine had her legs in Dylan's awkward duck-waddle stance as she stood at the standup organ, which she pretended was the urinal. The wrench Amandine had thrown in was that Dylan liked me watching him. "Come a little closer," Amandine-Dylan was saying in Dylan's nasal whine. "Don't be scared." I was trying not to laugh, to keep "in character," when the louvered door burst open.

"What are you girls doing in here?" Brett Lokler and Rudy Patrice stood in the door, smugly confronting us. They were in our grade, but cool enough to have perfected the sneer of upperclassmen, especially when they hung out together.

Shame burned through me. I stood silent, glued in place.

"We're studying," said Amandine, turning slowly to face the guys. Her hands moved to her hips. She looked bored and bothered.

"Oh, yeah?" Rudy sneered. "Sounds ved-dy in-ter-est-ing from outside the door."

Amandine shrugged. "If trying to memorize *Antony and Cleopatra* is interesting."

"If you're doing work, then where's your books?"

With showy deliberation, Amandine pulled a piece of paper from her pants' pocket. "Cheat sheet," she said. Then in a tired voice, read, "'Now to that name my courage prove my title! I am fire, and air; my other elements I give to baser life.' See? And you better not say anything."

"You idiot, you could get expelled for a cheat sheet," said Brett, impressed.

"Gee, tell me something I don't know."

Rudy yawned. "Let's go," he said to Brett. "I don't know what's up with these two freaks. Bye, girls." He stretched the last word into a chiming song.

They left.

"What twerps." Amandine exhaled a thin laugh.

"Is that really your cheat sheet?"

"Scrap paper." Amandine held it out for me to see. All that was on it was her name in doodle script alongside a sketch of a ballet shoe and a few words from a French vocabulary list.

"Then how did you know to say that stuff?" The freshman class truly was studying *Antony and Cleopatra*, and most kids had hardly read it, let alone learned it by heart.

"If it's a play or a dance routine, I memorize it," she told me. "Even if I don't want to, it's like I have to. I guess it's from all the plays I was in."

I believed her, and was impressed. Amandine had saved us. Her grace under pressure was enviable. But afterward, I wondered whether kids did think that there was something freakish about Amandine and me, and I couldn't help but keep an ear close to the ground, listening for the stealthy crawl of rumors. I knew that Amandine didn't feel any of that and I tried to imitate her indifference, but it was hard.

That Friday, I was staying at Amandine's house. I would be getting into the low red car. I would meet the face that belonged to the snappish voice of Amandine's father, whom she called Roger or Dad, depending. I would be having dinner at the gated mansion, which I pictured having stone fireplaces and mounted elk heads and a pool table.

After school, we stood by the curb together and passed the time doing skits.

We did a skit where Mark Ingersell asked me to the school dance, and he shows up at my front door wearing a mouth-guard retainer.

We did a skit where I had to accept a ride from our classmate Meggie Riet's snobby mom, and I have dog mess on my shoe.

"Sweetie," said Amandine as Mrs. Riet, her hands on a pretend steering wheel as she wrinkled her nose and looked over at me. "Have you been eating prunes? You smell a bit overripe. You know, the best prunes are imported from Persia."

I was laughing so hard I had to sit down. I could never keep in character. Maybe Amandine did it on purpose. She always seemed to know what to say to crack me up. It was one thing that I tried to hang on to when everything else made me want to forget all about her; that I never laughed so hard as when I was with Amandine.

Eventually, we got tired of skits and collapsed on the sidewalk in a fit of boredom. All the buses had left, and the parking lot was almost empty.

"Should we call?" I asked finally.

"No point," she answered.

After almost an hour more of waiting, a

car drove up. It was not the low red car, but a regular blue parent-y looking one. A rabbit-faced woman beeped and signaled.

"Where's Dad?" asked Amandine, opening the front door. I climbed into the back.

"Roger is having trouble keeping on top of his one responsibility as your chauffeur," the woman answered. "Hi, Delia, nice to meet you. He went over to Amherst to get some antique parts for his installation piece, and now he's stuck waiting for something, I didn't really listen. I mean, if you even want to believe him . . . and of course I was right in the middle of pouring a mold when he called, so . . ." her voice trailed off into a sigh of irritation. I noticed that her arms were crusted in gray chalk.

"Sculpting mud," she said when she caught my eye. "I'm Roxanne, by the way. I'm Amandine's mother." The light changed to green and she slammed on the gas. We shot through the intersection and careened onto the entrance ramp.

Amandine made a show of putting on her seat belt for safety, and for the rest of the drive we were silent.

Years ago, I was given a Halloween pop-up book. *Frightful Fun!* promised the title. It had only one page, just open the book and—pop!—an entire house sprang to form instantly, bisected so that you could see inside and examine all of its tricks. Every room had a coffin door or trapdoor or revolving door that revealed its secret vampire, goblin, or ghoul.

Amandine's house reminded me of that book. Its first trick was that it popped up out of nowhere at the end of a country road; a big gray haunted house set on a weeded lot and enclosed by an iron gate. Inside, there was no furniture, or hardly any. An um-brella stand in the entrance hall was filled with rolled-up, unread newspapers still in their blue plastic sleeves, and a cell phone plugged into a battery recharger was propped on the floor.

To the right and left of the large, square hall were a dining room and a living room, both still hung in the flocked wallpaper and massive curtains left over from a different kind of house. There were darker squares in the wallpaper where portraits and mirrors had been removed. Dusty glass chandeliers hung from the ceiling.

It was strange and exhilarating. When I stepped over a squeaky floorboard, I half-expected to fall through the trapdoor set beneath my feet, a quick dark drop to the goblin down below.

"We keep these rooms empty, for Art," said Amandine. She made a flying leap, or a "grand jeté," as she had told me it was called. "That's all my parents' work." Her finger swept back and forth, searchlight-style, indicating.

Now I noticed a couple of large canvases propped against the walls. Hands behind my back, I inspected more closely, as an art patron might. It was abstract art, the kind that made me feel stupid and tricked. In a corner of the dining room, I found something more understandable, a piece of sculpture that looked like a gate. The point-ended slats of the gate had been turned into animal ears, with woodcut animal faces fixed beneath. Deer, maybe. Or foxes, or Siamese cats. It was hard to tell.

"That's from Dad's 'Picket Fence' series," said Amandine. "A lot of his sculptures are about the dangers of the suburbs. About deer getting hit by cars and stuff."

"Jin made nutmeg cookies," said

Amandine's mom, whom I did not want to call Roxanne. I liked using Mr. and Mrs. They were like name shields to keep the adults back in their correct, distant places. "I'll be down in my studio."

"Who's Jim?" I asked.

"Jin, not Jim," Amandine corrected. She sniffed. "He always burns them. My room's on the third floor, at the top like yours, only we've got a whole other floor in between. Obviously, a really, really rich guy used to live here before us. Let's go."

Dust lay heavy as fleece on the edges of the stairs, in the corners of doors and windowsills, but I tried to hold my nose so that I wouldn't sneeze. It seemed rude, as if a sneeze pointed out how the house was in need of a cleaning. Doors to most rooms were solidly shut, but through one that was slightly ajar, I glanced in on a bedroom partially furnished with a mattress. On the floor beside it was a suitcase, open and scrambled with clothes.

"There's a back stairs, too, for the servants," Amandine said as we rounded the second floor. Implying that there were a few lurking around, which I doubted.

Amandine's attic room was regular, maybe even shabby. A worn quilt covered her bed, and the floor could have used a carpet, but a very nice entertainment system was set up on her bookshelf.

"That's Jin's," she said when I ran my finger admiringly over one of the speakers. "I'm keeping it for him while he lives here."

"Is Jin the . . . servant?" I asked.

"Don't be horrible," Amandine replied. "Jin is my mom's boyfriend. I told you about that, about my parents only being together for convenience, on account of me. Jin's an artist, too," she continued smoothly. "His studio's in the carriage house." She started to laugh. "I'm gonna tell him you thought he was a servant! That'll make him sooo mad!"

"Oh, no! Please, please don't tell him that." I sat on the edge of her bed. I felt a little bit sick. I thought of my own room, my prairie curtains and matching dust ruffle, my books and my cigar box of treasures and my bedside lamp that had three different light settings.

"I might have to go home," I said.

Amandine frowned. "But you just got here." She stared at me so intently that for a moment, I thought she was going to cry. Instead, she coaxed. "Come on, Delia. Jin's nutmeg cookies, the not-burned ones, are really good."

It depressed me that this was the best she could offer.

Roxanne did not come up for dinner. It was Jin who prepared it and then sat down to eat

it with us. A cauldron full of pasta in to-
mato sauce, garlic bread, and dumplings.
Lots of *stahch*.

Amandine flitted and hopped, filling
paper cups with soda water, retrieving napkins, ice, another fork. She chatted with Jin;
he told her about his day in the studio, and
then Amandine offered up a little bit about
what we did at school. Just snips of things
about math and how boring science data
sheets were, while Jin listened politely.

It was the fact of Jin that was harder to
believe.

Roxanne's *boyfriend*, Amandine had said.
But he was so young. Twenty-three? A little
older than college was my guess. He was
thin like a kid, and ate in huge mouthfuls like
a kid, and wore college-type clothes. The
cotton fabric of his T-shirt and baseball hat
were whiskered with age and his jeans rode
low on his hip with no soft stomach rolled

over the top like most dads. He was handsome, too. Polynesian on one side, Russian on the other, he told me. His face was angled and fluted. When he talked, his hands were all over the place gesturing, making even the smallest story exciting.

He acted the way I'd always pictured Ethan, my perfect pretend big brother. Jin was perfect, except for the fact that he was Amandine's mother's boyfriend, which made him weird.

Roger came home toward the end of dinner. A back door slammed and then steps thudded down to the basement—his studio, Amandine told me, was also in the basement, same as her mother's—and then pounded up again.

"Finally," said Amandine, rolling her eyes at Jin, who rolled his eyes back. "My dad," she said to me, as if it needed clarifying.

If I hadn't known beforehand, I might

have guessed Roger was Roxanne's brother instead of husband, or ex-husband, or whatever he was. Like Roxanne, he was spectacled and pointy and small.

"Hi." Roger's face twitched, he looked surprised to see me. I noticed he was wearing a scientist's lab coat. There were smudges of dried red paint on the elbow, giving him the look of a mad scientist who had just finished up some secret bloody experiment. He picked up a plate and loaded it with pasta.

"I told you Delia was coming," Amandine reminded.

"Yeah, I know, I know. I just forgot." Roger ate leaning against the kitchen counter, his legs crossed at the ankle.

"That you, Rodge?" Amandine's mom seemed to have flowed in from nowhere to become the center of the room and everyone's attention. "Finally. I hope you got what you wanted, after interrupting my entire day." She kissed Amandine on the top of her head, patted Jin on the shoulder, and didn't seem to notice me at all.

"Don't worry about it," said Roger, serving himself an extra helping.

"We have a guest, Roger," said Jin, inclining his head toward me. "Easy on the food."

Roger grunted; his head shook off Jin's remark like an old horse shakes off a fly.

Roxanne poured herself a glass of soda water and plopped into a seat at the table, her chin in her hands. I watched her. Everyone else was watching her.

"I can't get the color right," she said to no one, to all of us. "Too much green, too much white. What does April feel like?"

"You," said Jin.

I don't know why, but I blushed.

"She's talking about a painting," explained Amandine.

"She's always talking about a painting," snapped Roger.

"If you want to tell me I'm self-centered, then come out and say it," said Roxanne in a voice that was too loud for the room. "Be brave, Rodge."

Roger looked up at the ceiling and yawned.

"Delia, would you like some more pasta?" Jin offered the cauldron. I twirled a few thick ribbons of pasta onto my plate.

"Can we be excused to watch television?" Amandine asked.

I nodded agreement and set down my fork. I was suddenly, horribly, full. Stuffed.

The television was in what Amandine called the *solarium*, but this was another mostly empty room that was sunk two steps off the living room. A wraparound wall of windows took the place of wallpaper, and the television was propped on one of the deep sills, with pillows and blankets spread out on the floor in front of it. Amandine dropped onto her stomach and groped for the remote control. I dropped next to her. The blankets smelled musty and unclean. I contemplated going upstairs to Amandine's room to retrieve my sleeping bag, but decided against it. I didn't really want to wander through this house alone.

From far away, I heard a phone ring, and then I sensed that the other people in the house had crept off in different directions. An hour later, I thought I heard one of the cars pull out of the driveway. Nobody came in once to bother us or disturb us or to remind us to turn off the lights.

When I woke, cramped, to the iced air of early the next morning, the television was still on, muted to an early-bird cooking show. I felt a peculiar pressure and realized that Amandine's hand had locked itself around my wrist, five skeleton fingers handcuffing me. She was asleep, but I could see by the twitch of her closed eyes that she was having a bad dream. "I dare you, then!" she whispered once. Whether her body was tensed in fear or anger I couldn't tell.

I didn't know what to do, so I waited it out. When her grip eased, I tugged my hand away.

There was a small bit of fuzz on her cheek. I suppose I could have plucked it off with my fingers or ignored it, but instead, I leaned over her and lightly blew it into flight.

Amandine's eyes flew open and she slapped a hand over her nose.

"Delia!" she reprimanded loudly, outraged. "You should know better. Never, ever blow on someone's face. That is the grossest manners."

"I'm sorry," I said. "I didn't mean it to be gross."

"Plus, you have morning breath."

"Sorry, I said."

She rolled up onto her side and propped herself up on an elbow, facing me. "Delia, you're weird," she pronounced solemnly. "There is something wrong with you."

And she seemed so sure that it scared me a little. Probably I could have retaliated; there was a lot of weird, wrong stuff about Amandine, too. But to say anything seemed defensive and babyish.

The only thing to do was to smile in what I hoped was an uncaring way.

"How was the sleepover?" asked Mrs. Gogglio, the first thing out of her mouth when she picked me up for school at the beginning of the next week.

"Fine. Not too exciting. We had Italian food." It had become my stock answer, the one I'd given my parents. Because I had decided not to tell them anything about Jin and the Frightful Fun House, and the fact that we'd had cold leftover pasta and tap water for breakfast. It seemed like a secret and besides, what was the point? All that my parents would do was frown on Amandine and, worse, prevent me from visiting again. I doubted I wanted to, but it was my choice. My secret.

"Funny situation over there." Mrs. Gogglio's voice was conversational, inviting me to respond.

I glanced at her. She knew.

"You mean, with that . . . guy?" I threw and then slackened the line, waiting for her next tug.

"Mmm. Jim."

"Jin."

"Right. He lives there, you know. In that guest house or garage, but that's close as close gets. My friend Nancy Krause takes tickets at the Cineplex, she says they come in every Saturday night. The mother and her beau, and him barely out of some art school in New York City." Mrs. Gogglio clucked her tongue. "The times we live in."

"It's not as bad as it sounds," I said. "Everyone gets along okay."

"It's not natural."

"He's nice. Nice means a lot," I added, borrowing her phrase.

Her mouth pursed into a bud of doubt. But now I was glad Mrs. Gogglio knew about the Frightful Fun House. Otherwise, it all might have felt like a dream, something false and unsettling that I had made up in my head.

She changed the subject by telling me a

story about poor old Miss Benedict over at Sunrise Assisted, who kept a box of fabric scraps on her bedside table. The weekend duty nurse accidentally had emptied the box on Saturday, and Miss Benedict had sunk into a deep depression.

"I got the call yesterday," said Mrs. Gogglio. "She's been real blue. All that needs being done, I told Jenny—Jenny's on my routines for the weekend—all that needs being done is to replace the lost scraps with some new ones. You get to be as old as Miss Benedict, it's not about the actual things themselves, it's about hanging on to what you think is yours. Gives a person a sense of belonging to the world and vice versa, you see?"

I nodded. I could see that.

Spring fitness was scheduled Tuesday, Wednesday, and Friday afternoons. It was a class designed for the kids who did not play the "real" spring sports, which were softball, track, or soccer. The class was filled with kids like Eddie Patimkin, who used an inhaler, or Marissa Ruiz, who wore a back brace.

I took spring fitness by choice, because being on teams made me nervous, and Amandine took it because of her shinsplints. The class was supposed to satisfy the state physical fitness requirement, but I don't know how. We were always doing corny activities like square dancing or obstacle-course hopscotch. Things that didn't feel like sports at all. Still, I hated it—the damp-towel smell of the gym, the itchy nylon shorts we had to wear, the uncomfortable quiver in my stomach that lingered after the exercise was over. My face always heated up when I sweat, too, and Amandine would make fun of me.

"Wee wee wee, all the way home," was her joke. "That's you, Delia. You get as pink as a little piggy."

When Mom picked me up early that Tuesday for an orthodontist appointment, I was so happy to be getting out of spring fitness that I forgot to tell Amandine. It wasn't until I was in the car that it hit me.

"I need to go back in," I said uneasily. "I forgot something."

Mom's cheeks puffed in a show of impatience. "Is it absolutely dire?" she asked.

I thought. "I guess not."

"Because we're late already."

"Then forget it," I said, biting my lip. I didn't owe Amandine any explanation. She wasn't my boss. "Let's just go. Let's go."

For once, I had done something right.

"Everything looks wonderful," said Dr. Ang. She leaned forward across her desk and smiled from Mom to me and back again. Pretty and serene and a little bit remote, she did not seem to be the type to give compliments. But she was the type who had a passion for her job, and she stared admiringly at the X ray as she slid it to Mom. I could tell Mom did not want to linger over the ghostly imprints of my teeth.

"No, no, no," Dr. Ang reprimanded. "*Look* at it." She turned her attention to me. "You've been wearing the appliance for twelve hours a day, haven't you?"

I shrugged a yes. I'd hated having braces and welcomed the switch to a retainer, and I took all the precautions that would keep me from regressing to a mouthful of railroad tracks.

"You've made fine progress," said Dr. Ang. "Compared with the previous set of X rays that your dentist in Connecticut sent, it's remarkable. Remarkable." My mother's eyebrows lifted. Now she picked up the X ray and held it at arm's length, seeking out its hidden value as if she had just been told it was a Frank Lloyd Wright original blueprint.

"Delia's got a beautiful bite," said Dr. Ang.

An embarrassed tingling spread through me. It was rare to hear the word "beautiful" in the same sentence as "Delia." Even as I shrugged and pushed deeper in my chair, I wanted to go find a mirror so that I could stare at my beautiful bite in private.

"I *thought* it was starting to come along," said Mom.

As we walked out to the parking lot, she tugged a piece of my hair. "Good girl," she said. "See what you can do when you put your mind to it?"

It was the best my mother could do for a

compliment, so I took it as one. I am not one to ruin a happy mood.

The next day, when Amandine was not at my locker and I couldn't find her at lunch, I figured that she was absent. Entering the gym for spring fitness, however, I was surprised to see her and Mary Whitecomb sitting together on a pile of folded exercise mats and laughing.

"What's so funny?" I asked.

"We're just doing this skit," said Amandine. "I'm being Coach Frost and Mary has to rope climb and I'm looking at her underwear."

"How intellectual." I rolled my eyes, but my insides gnawed uneasily. "Where's Jolynn?" I asked Mary.

"Around," she answered with a roll of her shoulders.

Mary Whitecomb and Jolynn Fisch were

another pair of friends who took spring fitness. Amandine and I joined up with them when we needed to be a foursome for square dancing or baton relays. Mary seemed okay, but Jolynn scared me. She had a double-stud nose pierce plus a tongue pierce and wore aluminum-colored lipstick. Every afternoon she sneaked across the highway over to Holy Ghost Prep so that she could ride the bus home with her boyfriend, who was a sophomore there. Mary, who was vastly tall and had an underbite and wore thick scratched glasses, was less intimidating than Jolynn—though she did not seem as interesting, either.

And since when did Amandine do skits with her?

"We made up the skit yesterday," Amandine said, as if reading my thoughts. "When you were ab-sent." Her voice was accusing, slightly triumphant.

"Okay," I said. "Fine by me."

Then Amandine whispered something in Mary's ear. I edged away, unsure of what to do or where to place myself. This was my punishment, I knew, for being gone yesterday and not telling her.

Class got worse, as it was one of those rare days when Coach Frost decided to pick out partners himself, separating friends so that kids wouldn't cheat on that session's activity, which was a timed calisthenics test. But he paired Amandine and Mary.

My partner was Wendi Squires, who was a math whiz. She wouldn't round off the times on her stopwatch. "Delia, you can chin hang for eight point one six eight seconds," she announced. "One point eight three two more seconds would give you a perfect ten."

"Mmm." Out of the corner of my eye, I watched Amandine and Mary whispering endlessly in each other's ear. When I checked on Jolynn, who was paired with Marissa Ruiz, she didn't seem to care at all.

Suddenly, I found it hard to breathe, and in that moment I also desperately missed Lexi, and the easy friendship we'd shared back in Connecticut. A friendship that skipped across a week easy as checkers or Parcheesi, the same moves every time. Amandine's friendship was like a game of strategy, and it always reminded me how bad I was at strategy, and how much I didn't know.

Still, I kept quiet, waited. After school, it was as if nothing had happened. While we waited for our rides, we drew sketches of rotten eyeballs in Amandine's Ugliest Things notebook. Disgusting drawings were getting easier for me.

I didn't brave the subject until she called me on the phone that night. And even then I was careful, waiting for the right moment.

"What do you think about that girl, Mary?" I asked.

"She's all right," Amandine answered. "She's kind of a grub, but did you know she's in a fight with Jolynn? They don't speak to each other anymore."

I hadn't known, but I was used to Amandine noticing everything. "What's the fight about?"

"Jolynn's just a boy-crazy slut and Mary's had enough. I'm gonna ask her to sit with us at lunch tomorrow."

"Why?"

"Why not? I've been thinking, Delia. We really need a third friend. I mean, what happens if I'm ab-sent one day? Who are you going to hang around with?"

I thought about that. I saw myself wandering the halls alone. Sitting by myself in assembly. Pretty awful. But Amandine and Mary were in the same homeroom. What if they got to be better friends and started to share secrets and leave me out of stuff?

"Mary's dad's a minister," I recalled. "And she's sort of a priss, too, isn't she?"

"Don't be horrible. Just because she goes to church doesn't mean she's a priss. In fact, she was my computer lab partner last year, when we both were at James DeWolf Middle. She's *so* not prissy."

"Delia, you've been on that phone for over an hour," Dad said, startling me as he came out to the kitchen from the study. He was carrying his and Mom's empty tea tray, and I realized I'd forgotten to give them their nightly kiss. "Time's running . . . *out*." He said the last word like an umpire as he set down the tray and reached for the phone.

"Is that your dad?" Amandine squealed. "Tell him hi! Tell him I say, what's going on, old man!"

"It's Amandine," I said. "She says hi."

Dad misunderstood. He took the phone from my hand. "Hello, ballerina! When are you coming to fix our floors?"

There was a pause. Then Dad laughed.

"Oh, really?" he asked. And then, "What sort of tools and equipment might you need?"

A longer pause. Dad laughed again. "Of course, you'd be paid a working wage!"

Then Amandine said something else, and Dad's face lost its grin. "All right, miss. I'm saying good night from all the Blaines," he said. "Good night! Good night!"

He hung up the phone, his expression carrying faint amazement. "Miss Amandine," he said. "She's a real piece of work."

"Why, what'd she say?" I asked. "What'd that mean, about fixing our floors?"

"It was a joke she made up on the way to the hardware store, about turning the house into a dance studio, that morning I drove her home . . ." Dad looked troubled for a moment, as if he might tell me something more. But then he just said, "Okay, Honeydew, I'm turning in and so are you." His voice was loud, the way it had been on the phone. "Good night! Good night!"

The next day, Amandine asked Mary Whitecomb to sit with us at lunch. She brought extra food, I noticed—a half dozen of Jin's nutmeg cookies and a vending machine bag of Gummy Worms. She made a show of splitting everything into three equal parts. She was wearing a collared shirt, and her hair was rolled elaborately into two sausage curls pinned on either side of her face.

"It's my Joan Crawford from *Mildred Pierce* look," she told us. "A classic."

"It's nice," said Mary doubtfully.

"It's to make you think she's trustworthy," I said with a small laugh. Amandine didn't like that one. She glared, then sucked in her cheeks and looked past me, heavy-lidded.

"Oh, would you just get a load of Jolynn, sitting with all those guys. What a slut," she said with a sniff. I craned my neck. In fact, Jolynn was sitting in a mixed group of girls and guys.

Mary looked, too. "Actually, that's the debate team," she admitted. "They're competing against South Kenworthy High this afternoon. They're probably practicing."

Amandine arched her thickly penciled eyebrows and straightened her back. Her mouth downturned slightly, in an imitation of somebody I could not quite place. "You know what? You have a very pretty face," she said to Mary. "Contact lenses could change the whole essence of you."

Mary blushed. "Really, do you think?"

"Absolutely, dear." The imitation was of my mother. The same politeness, sincere and detached.

"Jolynn tried to set me up with Robby Verdone last year," Mary confessed. "He's a junior, he just got his license and a Vespa scooter. But it didn't work out. He's way too old for me. We went to the movies and I couldn't think of a thing to say all night."

"Robby Ver-*done*." Amandine wrinkled her nose. She would have said it about anyone, though. Amandine was not interested in the guys here, except to pluck as characters for our skits. In real life, they hardly seemed to exist for her. Not that I minded. Even gorgeous Mark Ingersell looked better from a distance. Up close, he made me feel sweaty and wrong.

"I'm taller than Robby, anyway." Mary frowned. "I'm taller than everyone. You guys know Jasper, my brother, he's on the varsity basketball team and *I* can hardly run three steps without tripping. Every time he sees me, Coach Frost probably thinks, there goes DeWolf's most humungous waste of arms and legs. 'Cause I mean, what's the point of being so tall if I can't even play basketball?" She was speaking fast, angrily, as if she had given the subject a lot of thought but had reached no peace with it.

"Delia's big brother, Ethan, plays running back on the football team at Washington State, and she can't do any sports, either," said Amandine. "And she's not even that much of a brain. She's just regular."

I'm in advanced math and English, I thought, but there seemed no point in mentioning it.

Mary looked at me with wistful empathy. "Isn't it awful? When the brother gets it all?

My parents always compare me and Jasper."
She looked so defeated that I was quick to
say the thing I know she needed to hear
most.

"Mine, too."

In the back of my mind, I knew that our
three-way friendship wouldn't last, but our
brief togetherness was a welcome break.
Amandine could be intense, yet Mary
seemed able to stand in Amandine's heat
without feeling the burn. And now I was
allowed to sit in the shadow, to observe quietly. Which was fine by me.

Mary shared her lunch with us every day.
She often brought us homemade foods,
brownies or cupcakes, treats far better than
anything Amandine or I could offer.
Sometimes she joined in the skits, but our
skits didn't amuse Mary the way they got to
me. Too often, usually right at the point

when Amandine had thrown in her wrench and revealed that her character was a pervert, freak, or snob, Mary would break out of character and shake her head disapprovingly.

"You *guys*," she would say. Or, worse: "I don't know how you talked me into these . . . story-plays. It's the stupidest kid stuff. I mean, we're *freshmen*."

She probably had a point, though I wished she wouldn't keep making it. When I peered down the halls or across at the other tables and desks, I didn't see other kids doing skits. I didn't see Samantha Blitz and her crowd living in a world of imagination and improvisation and make-believe. Everyone else was interested in beer and concerts and staying out and hooking up. Then I felt ashamed of myself, and I wondered what was wrong with me, why I couldn't be normal, and what Amandine had spied in my character that made her know that.

But Mary was normal enough. Mary was sweet, too. One morning, she arrived at school with a handful of woven friendship bracelets that she had made over that weekend. Mine was purple and white. Amandine's was pink and white. Mary's was pink and purple and white.

"I should wear the three-colored one," Amandine suggested. She did not explain why. Simply held out the flat of her hand.

"No way." Mary grinned. "It takes double time when you braid in the extra color. I'll keep mine, thank you."

I could tell that Amandine didn't appreciate that. If it were up to me, I probably would have handed over the nicer bracelet, just as I usually let Amandine have her choice of skits or the last word. This was a difference between Mary and me.

"Come on," said Amandine. "You can make yourself another one."

"Nope."

"How about I borrow it for the week and give it back?" Amandine persisted.

"How about no way, forever?"

"You can wear mine today," I appeased, taking off my bracelet and offering it up. "Then you have all the colors."

"All right." So Amandine wore two bracelets, and I wore none, and although Mary was irked by my solution, I'd solved the spat temporarily. It was part of my role, as a member of the group, and I wasn't bad at figuring out the thing to say or do to keep the peace. But I was not always there to tamp out the fires.

Since Amandine and Mary were both in the same homeroom and as neither of them was in the honors track, they shared a majority of classes. That meant lots happened in their day that I didn't witness. So if Mary did or said something that Amandine chafed against, I had to hear her complaints after school while we waited for our rides. It was always something—that Mary hadn't let Amandine cheat off her paper during a pop quiz, or that Mary forgot to save Amandine a seat in lab or study session.

One afternoon, Amandine walked up to my locker looking furious. Her face, usually so flat and still, was plummy with rage.

"You might be right that Mary's a stupid bitch," she said, whisking past me without stopping.

Quickly, I collected my books, slammed my locker shut, and followed Amandine out the doors. "I never said that."

"Did so."

"I said *priss*." My face was hot. "And I never said stupid, and whatever I did say, I said it a long time ago." I dropped my bag and crossed my hands over my chest, trying to get her to look at me.

"Fine, whatever."

"What happened?"

"Nothing."

"Really, tell me."

Amandine pressed a hand over her eyes. I knew she was nowhere near a state of crying, but I suspected she was trying to force it. When she lifted her hand, her eyes looked shiny, and I felt almost as bad for her as if the tears had been real. Tears are powerful, even phony ones. "The thing is," she began in a tremulous voice, "in art, I passed her a note asking her to draw a picture of her Ugliest Thing, and listen to what came back. You won't believe it."

She pulled an origami-style folded sheet of paper from the zip pocket of her book bag and then, in a voice that was too squeaky-mean, but otherwise not a bad imitation of

Mary's, read, "'Why would I want to draw an ugly thing? There are so many beautiful things in the world! Believe me, it's not good for the soul to celebrate ugliness! P.S. Did you take my bracelet? I put it in my desk before math and now it's gone. P.P.S. I promise I won't be mad. P.P.P.S. Here's a picture of you.'"

"That doesn't seem so awful," I said. "Can I see?"

"What, you think I'd make it up?" She flipped it to me. The picture of Amandine was just a stick figure in a tutu and ballet slippers.

I passed it back. "It's a little prissy," I admitted. "Like, using the word *soul* especially."

"Prissy? It's worse than a sermon! She probably copied it off her preacher dad!"

"Maybe she couldn't think up a good Ugliest Thing."

Amandine seemed to consider this. "No," she said finally. "She saw it as a way to slam me. Oh, and I like that extra touch, accusing me of stealing." She looked at me and stuck out her tongue. "Which we both know is *so* not true. Right?"

"Right," I answered.

"Are you with me for my joke, to get her back?"

"What kind of a joke?"

"Leave that up to me, how about."

I said nothing.

"Are you with me?"

"I guess."

"It'll be funny. I promise."

In my opinion, the worst thing about what Amandine did to Mary next was that she waited a day. To me, that seemed more awful than the "joke." The next morning, as I held my breath through classes, then through lunch, art, and fifty excruciating minutes of freeze tag at spring fitness—the only class I shared with both of them—Amandine acted as though she weren't angry at all. She chatted, shared lunch, passed around her box of lemon throat drops, even braided Mary's hair while they sat on the exercise mats once both of them had been tagged out.

She'd forgotten. I tried to convince myself.

"You look tired, Delilah," Mrs. Gogglio informed me on the ride home that afternoon. "What kind of day did you have that put such a sag in you?"

"Just a regular one, I guess."

"Munchkins?"

"Sure."

"I had my coupon book around somewhere. Do you see it? It's got a green felt billfold sleeve."

My heart was beating so loud I was sure

she could hear it. At that moment, all I wanted was to get out of the car and be alone, far away from school and Mrs. Gogglio.

"No."

"Oh, it doesn't matter. It wasn't much off anyhow. Fifty cents, if that."

We pulled through the Dunkin' Donuts and split a baker's dozen along with large hot chocolates. I closed my eyes and let the taste absorb me. Powdered, cinnamon, chocolate. Sweetly filling. It made me sleepy.

"Mrs. Roe, she forgot her own daughter's name today," Mrs. Gogglio began comfortably as she sipped her hot chocolate. "It wasn't unusual, but this time her daughter was there to see. 'Julie,' I said to her later, 'what's in a name? Your mama knows who you are without her needing to sticker a word onto your face.' But Julie was upset.

We were school friends, Julie Roe and I. Her mother used to dress up as a witch every year when she passed out candy on Halloween. Full of life and fun, Mrs. Roe was."

I listened, tried to loosen myself into Mrs. Gogglio's stories.

"You could talk to me, if you ever wanted," she said when she stopped the car at my driveway. "I'm just across the road here. I'm a pretty good talker, but I'm a five-star listener."

I nodded mutely and looked down at the front of my shirt. Powdered sugar had scattered all down the front. When I wiped at it, the powder turned streaky, making the mess worse.

The next morning, I almost stayed home from school rather than face another day of waiting and watching.

"You don't look sick to me." Mom's forehead rippled perplexedly. She checked her watch, smoothed her cuff over it, and tapped her low-heeled, business-casual foot.

"Maybe I will be."

"Up, up, up."

She flipped back the covers and left my room. I noticed that the flowers bought in honor of Amandine's visit had turned brittle and brown in their vase.

At school, Amandine met me at my locker. She was in a slinky dress too light for the weather. With a silky scarf and open-toed shoes and an anklet. She twirled.

"I'm Barbara Stanwyck today," she said. "From *Double Indemnity*. With my dragonfly pin, it would have been perfect."

"If you say so." I glanced her over. She looked ridiculous. Her dress smelled mildewed and her red lipstick was dry on her mouth. But her smile was smug, satisfied, and I knew that whatever she had done, was done. My stomach rolled.

"Is Mary here?" I asked.

"What do you need to tell her that you can't tell me?"

"You're not still mad at her about that note, are you?"

Amandine shook her head. "Not anymore."

I peered into the other homeroom on the way to mine. Mary was sitting alone at her desk. When I hissed her name and waved, she stared and didn't wave back. As Amandine pushed past me into the room, Mary looked down.

What was done was done.

I tagged Mary down in the hall after first period. Hooked her arm as she brushed by. She veered up like a spooked horse and nearly caused a couple of girls to collide into her from behind.

"Watch it," one girl snapped.

Which spooked Mary even more. Wheeling away from them, from me, she changed course and fled around the corner. I followed her into the sports locker room, which was empty.

"Go away, Delia," she called over her shoulder.

"Mary, what is it?"

She had pulled herself up into a huddle on the windowsill. Her overlong arms were wrapped around her knees with her nose buried into the space between. All I saw was hair. I stopped at what seemed to be a polite distance. From far away, the starting second period bell rang. I would have to be late to algebra.

"What?" I stepped from one foot to the other. "What?"

"That picture." Her voice was muffled.

"Picture?"

"As if you don't know!"

"Where is it?"

"What do you care?"

"I do. What was the picture of?"

Mary looked up, her face working hard to stay controlled. "You thought I'd throw it away, but I've got it. In case I want Mr. Serra to suspend you guys. It's evidence, you know. Bet you never thought of that."

"It wasn't me, Mary. Whatever it was, it wasn't me."

"Ha, ha. Funny, funny. You even signed it, in your own handwriting." She stared at me hard, then leaned back to fish inside her front jeans' pocket. The paper she extracted had been folded prettily in an imitation of Mary's own style. But the paper itself had the same thick creamy weight and texture as a page from Amandine's Ugliest Things notebook.

I unfolded it.

Amandine had used my rotten eyeballs as starting point. She had encased them in a pair of thick scratched glasses and gone on from there. In her picture, Mary was monstrously tall and hunched and hulking, a nightmare of all the things most awkward about her. Her underbite pushed her chin out like the man in the moon; the knobs of her elbows and knees stuck out from the church choir robe in which Amandine had dressed her. The details were scrupulous; the three-colored friendship bracelet, the scuffed hiking boots that Mary always wore, her carrot-shaped fingers. Amandine had picked up on everything and had translated it into this creature.

Our names were signed at the bottom— Delia Blaine, Amandine Elroy-Bell—under the neat capital letters that read:

MARY WHITECOMB:

THE UGLIEST THING AT

JAMES DEWOLF HIGH SCHOOL.

What made it bad was that it was so good.

"You're smiling." Mary snatched the paper.

"No."

"It's not anything to smile about."

"No, I know."

"Why did you?"

"I didn't. I mean, all I did was the eyeballs," I explained. "That's why I signed my name. She did all the rest. She made the rest of you out of the eyeballs." It sounded like a lie. I could hear my breath, shallow as a dog's. Why couldn't I ever say the right thing?

"I'm sorry," I told her, "but I promise, I really didn't have anything to do with this picture of you, Mary."

"That picture is not *me*," said Mary.

"No, of course not, all I meant was . . . Please, I promise we can clear this up." My voice whined, begging her. "We'll go find Amandine. She can't . . . she'll answer for it. She'll have to. She'll have to apologize."

It was lunch or never. I pushed through the rest of my morning's classes in a fog. It had taken some convincing, but Mary had agreed to meet me in the cafeteria so that we could brave Amandine together.

Fury and fear squeezed into a knot inside me. I just hoped that Amandine would be reasonable. That she would see how her joke had struck too hard. That she would understand how she had not thought all the way through the consequences. When she realized she had hurt both of us, she would back down. She would apologize. Amandine was tricky, sly. But she was no monster.

Spying her across the lunchroom, I relaxed. She was eating alone at our usual table in the back, her musty movie star dress flowing onto the floor under her chair, her back and shoulders ballerina straight. She looked almost pretty, certainly harmless. A water sprite, Mom had called her. Yes, I saw that.

"Hey," I began, forcing a false brightness into my voice as we approached. "Tell Mary that I didn't do any of that drawing."

Amandine looked up, startled, and her face tightened. When she spoke, though, she sounded only puzzled, and not at all defensive.

"Of course you did, Delia. It was your whole idea."

"Come on, Amandine. That's just a huge lie and you know it."

Amandine sighed patiently. Her eyes moved from me to Mary and back again. She pushed away her lunch and clasped her hands together to her chest as if in prayer.

"Mary," she began seriously, "I know it's

not nice for me to repeat what other people say behind your back, but in this case, I have to. When I showed her the note, Delia said, and I quote, 'That stupid prissy preacher girl only has to take a look in the mirror to find an Ugliest Thing.' See, and that's how the whole idea got started. The reason Delia's mad now is cause I actually showed it to you. The original plan was that we were just going to draw it for ourselves. I stuck it in your locker because she dared me for five dollars, and now I *am* sorry. Especially since Delia decided to *blame* me for the whole thing." She tipped her head in my direction and gave me a grave, wounded look. "Delia, I think I'll give you back that five dollars. It just wasn't worth it."

Mary backed away, her hands twisting. "I hate you both!" she said. "Both of you! I'd rather be marooned on a desert island than spend another second with either of you!"

Turning her back on us, she fled stumbling from the cafeteria.

I stared at Amandine, too shocked to speak.

She picked up her sandwich and bit into it contemplatively. "Marooned on a desert island," she repeated, giving each word scoffing emphasis. "If that's not the absolute lamest, prissiest thing I ever heard."

My fingertips touched my forehead. My brain felt gummy, slow to make sense of what Amandine had done.

"You," I began. "You." It seemed like the right word to start off with. "You are the worst, worst liar."

"The best liar, you mean. Don't be jealous. You're the best thief. How long have you had her bracelet, anyhow?"

"I did not steal Mary's bracelet."

"Of course you did."

"You made that up." I laughed uneasily.

"You never stop making things up, do you?"

"Oh, Delia, you're such a hypocrite. I could even tell your mother where it is. One phone call to Shelton-McCook—not that I'd ever do that. I don't care about any of your little stolen things." Her voice changed, became gentle and entreating. "It's no good with Mary and us, anyhow. She's always wrecking skits and being horrible. She's starting to talk about guys too much. And that *note*, ugh. I'm sick of her. Aren't you sick of her, Delia?"

My memory circled and returned to the morning that Amandine had stayed over. My bookshelf, my cigar box. She hadn't taken anything from me. But she knew.

"Sick of her?" I asked vaguely.

"Yeah, don't you think it's better, just us?"

"I guess," I said.

Amandine grinned. "Good. And now that it's just us, you have to admit it."

"Admit what?"

"That my picture of Mary was pretty funny. Wasn't it? Wasn't it?"

I nodded. "Yes," I answered. It was.

Mrs. Gogglio and I did not speak during the ride home, not even when she noticed that I was crying. I'd heard her make a quiet, sympathetic sound, and my whole body clenched against the questions I knew she wanted to ask. When she asked me nothing, I was grateful. She understood I was not able, not ready to talk yet.

"I'm just across the road," she said as I opened the car door.

I nodded, then ran up the walkway to my house. Free. Neither of my parents would be home for another couple of hours.

Relieved to be alone, I toured slowly

through the rooms. First my parents' downstairs, then my upstairs. Everything was neatly arranged under my mother's precise hand. Pillows plumped, this month's magazines in the wooden rack. There was aspirin in the medicine cabinet and there were fresh herbs in the kitchen window. It was nice here. Anybody could come into this house and feel at home, or at least as at home as I felt.

The upstairs was as tidy as the downstairs. Maybe that's why it didn't seem as if it belonged to me. I noticed that the wastepaper basket was empty, that my mother finally had thrown out my flowers. She swept through my room every few days or so just to make sure I wasn't hoarding snacks or storing up a collection of empty glasses and mugs.

But she did not know about my treasures. Neither of my parents did. It would not even have occurred to them to look. Somehow, though, it occurred to Amandine.

I did not hesitate. I took the cigar box from my shelf and headed over to Mrs. Gogglio's. My mind was empty. When I stepped onto her porch, I heard wind chimes, and my mind filled with their same erratic, tuneless clink.

She opened as I knocked. She must have seen me from across the way.

"Delilah! I'm having tea. Do you want some tea? Do you like cinnamon toast? I was fixing some for myself."

"All right."

"You have a seat in the front room there. I'll be right out."

I sat. Mrs. Gogglio's house was nice in a different way from ours. It was soft and faded and filled with things my parents would have rolled their eyes at; dressed-up mice dolls and framed Dolly Dingle pictures and netted lace everywhere—in the curtains, on the pillow fringe and lampshades. When Mrs. Gogglio came back and set down a tray, I saw that the tea set had a Popeye motif. Knock-kneed Olive Oyl danced with Bluto on the kettle. Li'l Swee'Pea beamed woozily from the creamer.

"Cream and sugar?" she asked.

I nodded. My mouth tasted metallic, as if I'd bitten it and drawn blood.

Watching Mrs. Gogglio pour tea was relaxing. She took extra care. Two sugars, cream. Stir, stir. Clink, clink.

My treasure box was opened on the coffee table. We blew on our tea together, sipped, and stared at it. I put down my teacup first. She lingered over hers. I had not bothered to hide the double-coupon book. In its green felt sleeve, it perched on top of Amandine's dragonfly pin. Other treasures, Mary's friendship bracelet, a fountain pen that had belonged to a teacher at my old school, lay in a jumble.

"I'm listening," she said. She placed her winking Popeye cup on his saucer.

"I've got these things," I began slowly. I stirred my fingers over the box, then let them fall on my favorite treasure, a cigarette lighter I'd had for so long that I couldn't even remember who it had belonged to before me. "And some of them aren't mine." I cleared my throat. "What I mean is, they all belong to people I like. People who have a lot—to offer, I guess. And I guess I feel like if I can take a chip off that person, just a tiny little chip, then part of what they have becomes mine. But it doesn't, really. It's just some dumb, stolen piece of nothing." I pushed my hands through my hair. I was raw, my insides turned out.

"And you're here because you think you're ready to stop holding on to these things?" she asked. Her voice was soft, her rosy apple face serious, trying to make sense of the information.

"Yes. Well, I'm not sure," I finished lamely. "It's something I've done for a while now. But it doesn't help me, or anything. It doesn't make me feel good."

Mrs. Gogglio thought on that a moment, then slowly she began to shake her head. "I'd never have missed that silly coupon book, Delilah. It was free in my mailbox, and the sleeve was free at my branch bank. So it's not for value that you took it. It looks to me that there's no real money value in any of what's there in that box."

"No."

"Then why did you want to show me this?"

Fear rose in my throat. It was suffocating me. I swallowed and braved it. "Mrs. Gogglio, you tell me these stories about old people, and all the things they do because they aren't in their right mind. Maybe I've got what they've got. Maybe I'm not in my right mind. All I want to be is normal, but maybe I'm not. Maybe I'm crazy."

I could hear the last words in the silence of the next moment, and it scared me. Was it true? Was I crazy?

I waited. The wind chimes clanked dully in my head. It was hard work to keep my seat, when all I wanted to do was to grab my treasures and run out the door and down the road to nowhere.

It was the nowhere part that held me in place.

"Odie MacKnight is ninety-six years old," said Mrs. Gogglio after a minute and another slow sip of tea. "His memory is failing him. He thinks he's back in the Depression. Talks about working as a hired hand. 'Gotta get to work,' he says to me every morning. 'Work or starve.' Makes me feel sorry for him, on account that he can only recall back to this sad time in his life. After the second war, he'd gone on to be an engineer. Married, bought a house ten miles away from here—his son lives in it now. Odie's got five children, eleven grandchildren, and a great-grandchild on the way. There's a lot to be thankful for. A lot of achievement in that life."

I stared at her uncomprehendingly.

Mrs. Gogglio smiled. "My way of saying it's a shame the most memorable time in Odie's history is the most painful. Just as I think it's a shame that you'll always have this time in your life to remember. Now I don't know much about the Depression, but I remember fourteen years old like it was last year. First time I saw you, I thought to myself, Why, now—there's fourteen! Oh, and it hit me like a train wreck, my memories of it. Good lord, I thought fourteen would never end."

She bit into her toast. I chewed my lip. Maybe it hadn't been such a good idea to come here. Mrs. Gogglio didn't really understand. I drew a shaky breath.

"What am I supposed to do?" I asked. "I don't know how to fix this."

Her face was a mask as she thought through my question, and I tried to find the fourteen-year-old girl in her features. It was hard. Mrs. Gogglio must have been more than sixty. "'One step at a time will make the whole journey.' Years ago, I read that across the back of a travelogue, and I never forgot it. I kind of adapted it into a life philosophy, if you know what I mean. Have you ever heard that expression?"

I shook my head. "No."

"Well, maybe you can borrow it as your own life philosophy for a little while. Maybe that's how you could think of each of these knickknacks. One step."

She reached into the box and held up Amandine's dragonfly pin, which I had taken during my sleepover. It was brass-plated, and one of the dragonfly's red glass eyes was missing. But I had liked the way it glittered in my hand. It had seemed to buzz when I held it, a secret buzz for me alone.

"Pick your steps," Mrs. Gogglio said. She replaced the pin in the box; then she took her green felt coupon book and slipped it in her pocket, out of sight. "There. I just helped you take your first one. And see, not so bad."

She leaned over and patted my knee with a flattened palm. "Of course you're in your right mind, Delilah. You're not crazy, not one bit. What I see is someone who's trying to make the girl she is match up with the girl

that other people want her to be. And sometimes she gets overwhelmed."

Overwhelmed. Well, that was true enough.

"How about another cup of tea? You like
this silly old tea set? It was three dollars at a
tag sale in Vermont. You know, I think you'd
like tag sales. Lots of people's funny odds
and ends, already with a bit of a history
rubbed off on them. We ought to go to one,
when the weather warms up."

One step at a time.

I had snitched Samantha Blitz's bandanna, and only gave it back to her when I
thought Amandine might have spied and
recognized it in my box of treasures. At
the time I hadn't been sure if Amandine
actually had discovered my cigar box and
peeked inside.

Now I was positive.

It was hard to give up the cigar box, itself

a treasure that I had smuggled out of Uncle Steve's den and into my suitcase during a visit a few years back. If Amandine knew about the box, though, I could not run the risk of keeping it around. After I came home from Mrs. Gogglio's, I dumped my treasures on my bed and stamped on the box to flatten it. Then crept to the kitchen, where I slipped it into a brown paper bag and buried it under the stack of newspapers that were twine-tied and ready for tomorrow morning's recycling truck.

Next, I gathered my loose treasures into a plastic freezer bag. The weight of the bag was comfortable, heavy in my hand. It would be hard to let go of all of my treasures. A lot of me didn't want to.

One step at a time. Every step was moving me farther away from Amandine. Closer to the side of the normal people. I could do that. I would do that.

I pushed the bag into my empty flower vase.

My second step would be Mary's bracelet. I'd already wrapped it in some tissue and placed it in my book bag. I hesitated for a moment after I tucked it there, letting my finger rub the bracelet through the paper's delicate skin. It didn't have to be now, I reasoned. Maybe I could hold on to it for another week. I had taken to wearing the bracelet while I did my homework, and it made me unhappy to think I would no longer see it sliding up and down my arm.

I purged the feeling from my thoughts. Unhappy now, to be happy later. Later, in a place where Amandine held nothing over me.

PART THREE

She was waiting for me at my locker the next morning. She was all I saw; it was as if everything else in the hall had sunk underwater. Shimmering walls and floors, the noises and faces of other kids were remote and blurred into the kind of incomprehensible motion that happens in dreams.

She shone like a bleak sun through my murky vision. She was dressed in innocence, all wispy whites and pinks. I blinked, trying not to stare at her directly.

"Hi!" she said.

I nodded. I was moving underwater. I could hear my own breath in my ears, in and out, diver-deep. My knees went weak from the forcible effort of walking purposefully closer to her.

"Hi!" she said again.

Again, I nodded. Now she was on my side, now she was past me. I walked without pausing, without a word I passed her by.

Amandine's eyes beamed on the back of my head. Disbelieving, flat, enraged.

I did not have to see to know.

Triumph rocketed through me and I allowed myself a smile. I did it. I'd done it.

Yes, I was stronger than I thought.

"I borrowed this," I told Mary. I set the tissue-covered bracelet on her desk. "I was going to tell you I found it or something, but that's not really true. The truth is I wanted to wear it for a while. But that was really, uh, . . . abnormal of me, I guess, and I'm sorry."

Mary looked up. She unpeeled the tissue and shook the bracelet over her wrist.

"Thanks."

"And I want to apologize for anything I did or might have done, and even for the things I didn't do that you think I did. I apologize."

"You should watch out, Delia, before you apologize away your whole existence," she said. I could not tell if she was joking or warning me. I nodded as if I understood. Her gaze flicked past me, my signal to leave her, so I did.

In my pocket was my step three—Rudy Patrice's sterling pound note coin that he'd brought back from his family's recent vacation to Europe. I sat at Rudy's homeroom desk for algebra, and it had been one of my most recent treasures that I had taken from

James DeWolf, only a week ago. Rudy had never talked about missing it; perhaps he hadn't noticed its absence yet.

In math class, I slipped the coin back, a solid clink of metal against metal as it hit the bottom of the desk.

"*Godspell* opens next weekend, over at the Walk the Plank Theater," Dad said that evening when I came into the den to say good night. "Mom and I were thinking that if we picked up four tickets, you could invite your thespian pal, little Miss Amandine."

"We're not friends anymore," I said.

"I see." Dad sighed. "Well. There goes that."

"I'm sorry," I told him, because I was, because now his spotlight had clicked off, leaving me standing alone in a dark place.

"Playing the loner is a lonely game, Delia," said Mom with the assurance of someone who believes she has said something very wise and true, only when I thought it over later, it wasn't either of those things.

With no more Amandine and no more Mary, I went from two friends down to none. My imagination had played worse tricks on me than what reality doled out. I guess that is usually the way. In my mind's dread anticipation, loneliness was a bullet, hard and abrupt, the shock and pain of being discounted.

In reality, loneliness was more like a slow and constant drowning. I simply disappeared. The hall and classroom swallowed me up, and I became invisible, my quiet flailing unnoticed. Same as it had been at my old school, only there I'd had Lexi, my lifeboat.

I tried not to keep tabs on her, but I couldn't afford not to be on guard against

Amandine. Without Mary and me, she began to hang around aggressively with Jolynn. She even came to school wearing lipstick and nail polish in the identical pewter color that Jolynn preferred. But as far as I could tell, Jolynn was indifferent to Amandine's tricks, and I could have bet that Amandine had nothing much to contribute to all that gossiping about guys and clothes and parties.

She was through with me. And I was sad. The truth was, school was boring without Amandine. The deep, outrageous thrill of being overwhelmed by a wave of laughter in assembly, or of opening a note filled with her whip-sharp jokes and drawings, or the wild excitement of a skit was all over now. The whole froth and churn of the day had gone flat.

Now Amandine hardly registered me. Sometimes she sent a vague nod in my direction when we passed in the hall, but I had hurt her once, deliberately, and once was enough. I asked Mrs. Gogglio to pick me up at a side door so that I could avoid waiting for my ride with Amandine.

Better to avoid her, I thought.

My one consolation prize was that for the very first time since I started James DeWolf, I was able to pay full attention in class. The focus paid off, and the next week I got my first A, in algebra.

"Wonderful," my parents praised me. "You're really adjusting well, Delia."

It was amazing to me sometimes, how much they did not see.

At the end of that week, a slip of paper fluttered from my desk.

Meet me for lunch in the sports locker room?—M.W.

Was Mary still angry about the bracelet? Did she want to see me so that she could have it out, a final slam before she went back to ignoring me, as she had been doing for these past days? It took my last nerve to collect my bag lunch and propel myself into the locker room after the first lunch bell rang. But I was so lonely that even Mary's anger seemed better than nothing at all.

Mary was wrapped up on one end of the windowsill, her sandwich and celery sticks spread out on a napkin on her lap. She waved when she saw me. I approached carefully.

"Sometimes I eat here on the windowsill when the cafeteria gets, um, too rowdy," she said. "It's more peaceful, see. Nobody comes in here during lunch. And I thought you might . . ." She gestured to the space opposite.

"Sure," I told her. "Thanks." I climbed up on the windowsill next to her, and we ate together quietly, our backs warm against the midday sun. Over the past couple of weeks, I had been skipping lunch, sneaking bites of things in the halls between classes and using the actual lunch time period to study in the library, where food was forbidden. I welcomed the change.

"Actually, I wanted to talk, for real," Mary told me, after we finished our sandwiches and had passed some time talking about easy things, like what we might be doing this summer. "I've got a problem."

"What is it?"

"Amandine," she said. "She won't leave me alone. She calls me on the phone, sometimes twice a night. She passes me notes. I just wish she would go away. If you want to know the truth, I'm kind of scared of her."

"Me, too," I said, trying to dismiss a twinge of sadness, because Amandine certainly was not calling me. She hadn't done any work at all to reclaim my friendship.

"And Jolynn and I aren't friends any-more," Mary continued. "So it's this funny situation. I don't know who else to talk to about her. But then I noticed you've been avoiding her, too, and I thought, okay then, maybe you and I had more in common than I'd figured? I'd wanted to be sure, since it seemed like the both of you were so close—it was hard for me to know if I could trust you."

I nodded. I tried to think of what to say, and settled on a smile.

"Also, it's been boring these past weeks, without anyone," Mary mentioned.

"Better to be bored than . . ." I raised my arm, a meaningless motion, but she got what I meant. Better to be bored.

"You know, you could come over some weekend, Delia," she offered in a rush. "We live way out, on a farm. We've even got a horse, Pegasus—Peggy. She's too old to ride but you can pat her. It's nice in the country."

"My uncle Steve says barefoot in green grass is as close to paradise as we mortals get," I told her. Mary nodded solemnly.

"Sounds like my mom," she said. "But you'll like them. My parents, I mean. They're not all Bible-ish, the way Amandine made them out to be—reciting dinner table prayers until the food's gone cold. They're totally normal, they let us watch rated Rs and go online just like regular parents."

I laughed. The sound was pure relief, a trickle of cold water through a parched riverbed.

Later that night, right in the middle of prime time television, she phoned.

"Honey, it's Amandine." Mom called from the kitchen. Shock buzzed my body. I had assumed from the conversation that I had been eavesdropping in on—all about flowers and rain and patio covers—that the caller must have been my grandmother.

Amandine's voice, a snake slithering into my home, catching me off guard. For nearly five minutes she had been here, chatting up my mother in that fake perky voice of hers.

"Delia?" Mom called again.

I pried myself off the couch and walked into the kitchen. I took the phone from my mother as she left the kitchen for the den. I slid against the kitchen door, the glass a support against my back.

"What?"

For a long minute, all I could hear was heavy breathing. I almost laughed out loud. What kind of stupid threat was that?

"For future reference, Amandine, when you're doing a crank call, it's more effective when you don't actually identify yourself to the person's mother and then talk to her for, like, ten minutes about gardens."

The breathing stopped. In the expanding silence, my courage failed. I could not let out my own breath, scared of what I would miss.

When she spoke at last, the voice she used was shiny and false. Her stage voice.

"You will pay, Delia."

My pulse raced. "What are you talking about?"

"I'm talking about you and Mary against me. You'll pay for it. I saw you guys together after last bell. Where were you at lunch? Did you have lunch together, too? Because if you think you can just be—be *against* me like that, you're wrong. Mary was my friend before she was yours. You stole her, like you steal everything. You're nothing but a plain old ordinary thief."

Mom bustled back in, eavesdropping politely as she rinsed her and Dad's tea mugs and placed them in the dishwasher. I had to be careful.

"It's not like that, Amandine," I said evenly. "It's just I think Mary's nice is all. She's really . . . normal." My pulse throbbed. It was sort of exciting, anyway, to have one over on Amandine, both of us knowing that Mary preferred my friendship to hers.

"You can consider this a formal threat, and your last warning. I'll see you tomorrow in the regular place by your locker. This is it, Delia. Your big chance. If you don't screw it up, I forgive you. Are we clear?" The line sounded rehearsed, as if she were stealing a piece of play or movie dialogue. I wondered if Amandine was as angry as she sounded, or if she was merely testing out the role.

It was impossible to know.

"Okay. See you tomorrow," I said casually, for my mother's benefit.

There was a click in my ear, a click that

I didn't fully register until it was replaced by the sound of an automated voice telling me to please hang up and try my call again. I hung up the phone carefully.

"She's the most charming little thing, that Amandine," my mother mentioned, turning to me from where she was at the sink, cleaning the trap. "Why don't you have her over again some weekend? I've been seeing advertisements everywhere for the spring fair over in Dalestown. That might be fun."

"We're not friends anymore," I said. "I thought I'd told you. I know I did."

"You seemed friendly enough on the phone," she said. Then she turned to face me. "Really, Delia. Just say you're sorry, no matter whose fault it is. That's how Dad and I do it. Then it's all over and behind you."

I nodded vaguely. No point in getting into it.

* * *

The next morning, I deliberately blew my big chance at Amandine's forgiveness by sneaking around the school's back entrance, cutting down the senior hall, then taking the back stairs and crossing through the library into homeroom.

As I hurried, I imagined her standing beside my locker, her lipstick a spot of color on her pale face and a new skit ready to offer like an olive branch. And I imagined her eyes turning hard and blank when she realized that I had tricked her.

Later, when I did catch sight of her in the hall, she ignored me as if nothing had happened. She was outfitted dramatically, in a cinched Spanish-style lace skirt and yellow blouse. Her red lipstick was bright as a fire engine.

I didn't know the movie, nor the role she was resurrecting, but I could tell that she was dressed for victory. For celebration. It made me feel guilty.

"Señorita Amandita," someone sang out as she ruffled past.

"What a weirdo," Mary pronounced later when we were eating lunch together in the windowsill. "That outfit! I'm surprised she didn't put a rose between her teeth."

When I related the gist of Amandine's call and threat last night, Mary had dismissed it.

"She's mental."

"The last thing I want to do is go back to being friends with her." I spoke with strength, but I knew that part of me, a secret part, missed Amandine. Wanted her back, with all her terrible fun.

"I've been going to school with her for three years, ever since she moved here from New York," said Mary. "She's never been able to find her right fit with this class. She'd be with someone for one month, someone else for another, and so on and so on. Nobody ever worked out."

"That's too bad," I said. "Adjusting can be hard for some people, I guess." My voice a touch smug, maybe.

"Hey, I meant to tell you. My mom was making a recipe out of a cookbook the other night and I found out. Do you know what Amandine means?" Mary grinned as I shook my head no. "If you prepare anything *almondine*, all it means is that it's made with almonds! Amandine's name almost means almonds!"

"Oh." That didn't seem like much information, but Mary loved it.

"Made with almonds!" She snorted. "Topped with almonds! I always thought it was a made-up name!" Mary was doubled over in laughter now, she seemed to think that this was really funny, and I tried to join along. But all I could think was that it wasn't the way I laughed with Amandine. No matter how hard I pretended it was.

That weekend, I stayed over at Mary's house. Her family was better than just regular, as she had described them. In my mind, they were perfect. The Whitecombs treated me as if I had been visiting their house for years.

After Mary showed me around, we walked around their land and fed Pegasus an apple, then prepared dinner for everyone—English muffin pizzas, with homemade cantaloupe sorbet for dessert. The sorbet didn't freeze right and was more the texture of cantaloupe soup, and Mary's brother, Jasper, teased us about it. Mary was right—Jasper really did "get everything." Not only was he handsome and athletic but he was also more at ease with himself, more confident than Mary.

Reverend and Mrs. Whitecomb didn't

favor him, though, not that I saw. There was room for Jasper as well as Mary, whom they all called Daisy because, as Mary blushingly explained, she had been such a big, clumsy kid that everyone said "oops-a-daisy" whenever she fell over or knocked something.

It seemed fantastic to me—a family who turned a flaw into a cute nickname.

After dinner, we watched horror movies and gave each other home spa treatments— mud masks and French manicures. My manicure looked mature and made my fingers seem as if they should be occupied with glamorous tasks. The spa stuff was fun, a different kind of fun than skits.

That night, tucked safe in one of the twin wicker-framed beds in her room, I finally confessed to Mary that I did not have a big brother. "It was one of those stupid things that started small and got bigger and bigger," I said.

"Another crazy Amandine idea," she answered knowingly, and I didn't deny it. While the lie of Ethan had been all mine, he did seem like Amandine's fault. Her own lies had forced me into making him up.

Another week passed, and Mary stayed over at my house.

"She's nice," Mom pronounced, Dad nodding his head in agreement. They offered nothing more. I figured they were secretly disappointed that I hadn't been able to keep my one exceptional friend. Clumsy Mary, nice as she was, had nothing on the kitten-faced girl who sang *Carmen* and danced *Coppelia*.

For me, it was different. I could relax around Mary. I even told her about my one sleepover at Amandine's, leaving out nothing, describing Jin and the Frightful Fun House and the pasta and water for breakfast. We laughed about it. Crazy Amandine.

What were we thinking, being scared of her? She was a freak, her family was abnormal, we should have known better.

I began to feel safe.

The next weekend, Mary stayed over at my house again, and my parents dropped us off at the fair out in Dalestown. We rode the Ferris wheel and Mary won a stuffed polka-dot snake at the shooting gallery, and then we called Mark Ingersell from a pay phone by the parking lot. I was supposed to talk to him, but after identifying myself to his mother as Diane Veers, the best-looking girl in our class, I could keep my nerve only until I heard his voice on the line.

"You hung up, shy-baby!" Mary giggled and pointed her finger at me. "Why?"

"What was I supposed to say?"

"Anything! Anything!"

I wasn't quite ready for the risk of *anything*, but I was moving closer. One step at a time to normal, and lately the journey seemed safer. Maybe even fun.

On Sunday, Jasper Whitecomb dropped me home, where I found my parents waiting for me on the front lawn. Side by side under a tree in their pair of lawn chairs, their iced teas resting on the matching glass-topped table between them. They waved as the Whitecombs' car drove up, shouted a cheerful thanks to Jasper, and waved again when he backed out and left. But there was something odd in the way they were seated, like judges, that made me feel nervous.

I knew they were waiting for me.

"We got a call early this morning from Roxanne Elroy," said Mom as I approached. "Your friend Amandine's mother. She was very upset. Your dad and I have been talking together all morning, and we haven't figured out any answers on our own, so we decided it might be best to talk to you." Her voice was polite, as if she had met me only a few hours ago.

"What did I do?" My heart was thrumming. There was no place to sit and so I was forced to continue to stand like a convict before them.

Dad shook his head. "Nothing, Delia. It has nothing to do with anything you've done. It's not about you." His voice sounded crisp and impatient.

"Well, that's not entirely true." Mom crossed her legs neatly, folded her hands on her knee, and continued. "Delia, how would you describe Amandine?"

"What do you mean?"

"I mean, she's your friend and—"

"But she's not my friend!" I burst out. "You've known that. I've told you that. She's weird. What did she do? What?"

"Delia, what does *weird* mean? Be more precise. This is serious."

"Weird, like, she draws these things . . . and she tells stories, and she likes to be nasty to people, she's nasty to me, I don't know what else. Weird. What else do I say?"

My father stood. He picked up his iced-tea glass and tossed its dregs and ice cubes into the flowerbed before retreating up the lawn to the house. He was wearing a regular brown leather belt, I noticed. The silly tie was gone. Mom and I watched him until he went inside, banging the screen door that he had recently installed.

"Is Dad okay?" I asked.

"He's tired." Mom rubbed her face with her hands. "It's been a long morning." Her eyes fogged over as she glanced at the flowerbeds. "It might be a while before we see zinnias," she said. Her voice was detached. "We're late to seed . . ."

I dropped into the empty chair. I was coldly perspiring.

"Please, Mom, tell me why Mrs. Elroy called," I said. "Tell me what's going on."

Mom glanced toward the house, and then began to speak very fast and methodically, as if she were performing some distasteful job that she wanted to get finished in a hurry.

"Apparently, your friend Amandine told her mother that your father had behaved inappropriately, that time he drove her home after she spent the night here. That he tried to . . . kiss her." My mother's laugh held no trace of humor. She tossed her head and flashed a pained hostess smile. One hand pressed against her chest. "Really, it's too stupid, it's not important, it's obviously not true. We are dealing with a troubled girl who is upset by something and she's lashing out and it's as simple, as transparent as that."

For a moment, I could not speak.

Disbelief dried up all the words inside me.

"She's worse than troubled," I managed finally. "I could give you a hundred different examples of worse. A thousand. That's why I'm not friends with her anymore. Believe me, please believe me. You've got to."

Mom hardly seemed to register what I was saying, speaking more to herself when she answered. "Roxanne Elroy has decided not to go to the school with it. She says there's no point in any kind of legal involvement. It's not a serious crime, she said, so much as a distasteful misdeed. Her words. Anyway, she requested that you keep away from Amandine."

"Keep away from her? I haven't even talked to Amandine in almost two weeks. It's ridiculous that she would tell such a huge, awful lie!"

"Ridiculous, vicious, wrong. And, evidently, her revenge on you for your falling

out, though that is hardly your fault, Delia."
She sighed. "You know, I do believe that if
we had been a week earlier on the zinnias,
we'd see blooms by the end of the month."

Mom now was reaching down to brush
her finger back and forth, back and forth
against a pale green shoot that was starting
to push its way into the sun. It was a signal
to me that she had finished her discussion
about this; or rather, her discussion with me
about this.

I sat there for a moment, unsure. Then
I stood and ran across the lawn, into the
house, and upstairs to the safe exile of my
room.

In spite of my mother's words to the con-
trary, I felt that I had done something
wrong. That Amandine, my Amandine, was
also my fault, and that I was partly to blame.

Amandine's lie was like the wrench thrown

into a skit. The skit was our fight, and her lie allowed her character, the character of "Amandine," to return to a familiar role.

Amandine, the innocent victim.

Amandine, who had suffered an injury at the hands of someone strong and cruel.

When I saw her at school the next day, all I wanted to do was to run up to her and shout that I saw right through the whole pathetic performance. I wanted to slap her. I wanted to hurt her back.

"Don't," my mother had warned me at last night's mostly silent dinner. "No matter how strong the urge is to confront her. It's not what we need and it wouldn't do us any good. A silly story like this has both the potential to be worse and the potential to blow over. Dad and I, for one, would prefer the second effect."

Numbly, I agreed. Maybe it was better to keep my distance. My public explosion was most likely exactly what Amandine craved. Over the next few days, I began to believe that she put herself deliberately in my path at school, to test me. So I kept my distance and acted nonchalant. If nobody else knew, then it was as if it hadn't happened.

Things were happening, anyway. First, I caught an unmistakably dirty look from Jolynn Fisch in spring fitness. The same afternoon, a cluster of whispering girls stopped talking and stared at me with slit-eyed scrutiny when I passed by.

Now everything fell under the shadow of my second-guessing. Why didn't anyone sit across or behind me in study period, the only class where seats were not assigned? And was that a contemptuous beat of silence after I had answered a question out loud in English class?

Mary didn't say a word about it, and I was too mortified to bring it up. Had

Amandine been telling everyone at school this creepy story? Or was I just imagining things? It became harder to convince myself.

I was in art class when the truth washed out. We were drawing at easels from a still life set out in the front of the room. Tipped-over coffee and tennis cans. My ovals were sloping like deflated tires and my paper was ragged with erasing. Over the past few days, it had become difficult to concentrate on anything.

"H-hey, Delia."

I looked up.

After so many skits, the real-live, up-close Mark Ingersell was a shock. His eyes, that had only locked mine when Amandine pretended to be him in skits, were different from the way I had imagined them. Not hard and gray, but blue and soulful. And I realized that I did not know Mark Ingersell at all.

"What?" My fingers clenched my pencil.

"Your dad's some kind of p-pervert, or what?"

"My dad?" My voice, like my coffee can ovals, came out raggedy and deflated.

"Y-yeah." His stammer was just the way Amandine did it. She was a great mimic. "I heard if anyone in y-your family comes inside twenty yards of that girl, Amandine, he gets hauled off by the c-cops. Is that r-right?"

"I don't know what you're talking about."

"Oh, yeah?" Thunderstorm blue. I hunched under his gaze. "That's n-not what I've been hearing." He paused, his face reflecting something between puzzlement and scorn, then turned and strolled back to his easel.

I looked over at Miss Rose, our art teacher who was stooped in a corner of the room, sorting acrylic from oil paint tubes.

She had no idea. I blinked down at my coffee cans. All the kids knew the story, I realized. All of them, every single one. The entire class had fallen into a hush when Mark approached me. Now, as I stared at my paper, I could sense their nudges and whispers.

After a few torturing minutes, I excused myself from art and spent the rest of class time hiding in the bathroom, tearing a piece of paper towel into a thousand little scraps and dropping each scrap one by one into the toilet.

The worst thing about school, any school, is there is no right place to go when everything goes wrong.

Spring fitness was my next class. I kept a careful distance while we hit tennis balls against the gym wall and I caught up with Amandine afterward, while she was changing in the sports locker room.

"Why are you telling everybody this lie?" I asked her. "You don't know what you're doing."

"You're not supposed to talk to me, remember, Delia?" Her voice projected loud, all the way to the back row of the theater, if we had been in one.

"This isn't a skit," I said. I held my arms crossed at my waist, my elbows squeezing hard against the sides of my body. "This is real life."

"True," she agreed. "This is real life. And if you keep on talking to me, my parents will get the real police involved."

A few girls standing near us had gone utterly silent.

I backed off, terrified. Amandine arched a pewter-penciled eyebrow and tugged off her gym shorts. Standing in her underpants, her exposed legs looked uncooked and undernourished.

She loved it. The audience was trans-fixed. We were all watching her.

Only late at night, wide-awake in the dark-ness, did I allow myself to think about this.

They are in the car and the music is on. Throughout the entire trip into town, they have been play-acting. His silly accents and her quick retorts make a happy banter between them. The sun glints behind her, standing her hair into a blond halo, and she is focused and sure in his spotlight. She is sophisticated and clever and pretending to be old for her age. She is nothing like me.

And that's why he kisses her. It seizes him in a fit, like in those old movies, when a kiss was something you had to have against all better judgment.

I sat up in bed, dry-eyed. "You liar. You lie about everything. Every single thing!"

My anger was lonely, though. It whispered through my room with no place to go, but I couldn't get rid of it.

Amandine's teeth once had reminded me of a kitten's, but I had chosen the teeth of the wrong animal. Because Amandine, the real Amandine, was slippery as an eel, and she attacked with an eel's unexpected, vicious bite.

It was done and there was no undoing it. The image of Amandine and my father might have been torn straight from her Ugliest Things notebook, was now pressed permanently into the pages of my mind.

Mr. Serra's office was clean and worn, like Mr. Serra himself. He sat tucked upright behind his desk. A fountain pen was balanced horizontally through his three middle fingers; he tipped it back and forth like a seesaw. He was a small, combed man like

Batman's Robin. A sidekick waiting for the real hero to arrive.

But there was no Batman. Just me and my mother.

After we had taken our seats in the two chairs facing him, Mr. Serra stood up and closed his office door.

His window showed off a boring view of the parking lot. I looked out anyway.

It was on my insistence the night before that my mother had called Mr. Serra. Outrage had made me brave. I would expose Amandine, I decided. I would plead my case and explain who she really was, and maybe everyone would understand that none of this was my fault, and maybe they'd even realize that it was I who had suffered most.

In the fresh glare of morning light, with my mother coiled like a spring in the chair beside me, my nerve faltered. I squinted into the sun. If I stared long enough, perhaps I would go blind. At least it would create a new crisis to stamp out the old one.

"Delia," said Mr. Serra. I turned. He looked as if he would rather be anywhere than behind his square steel desk. "This is a delicate predicament. The school is reluctant to take action, officially, as there has not been a formal complaint filed, and as whatever did or did not happen, did or did not happen outside the school's jurisdiction. But. In light of your current . . . dilemma, in that somehow this . . . story . . . has become . . . known, I am ready to hear what you feel you need to say. So, yes." He smoothed a hand over the back of his head, spent from his excessive speechmaking. Then he picked up a piece of paper and set it down without looking at it. "You think, it is your opinion, that Amandine Elroy-Bell is a . . . threat . . . to the . . . student body?"

"I know she's lying," I said with what I

hoped was an expression of the whole truth under oath. "She's lied before."

"Well, Delia, there are two sides to every story. Another version would suggest that maybe it is you who hasn't been playing as straight a hand as you might have." Mr. Serra put down his pen and laced his fingers together over his chest. "According to her mother, Amandine says you took things from her."

"*That* I know is nonsense." My mother raised a hand to stop Mr. Serra from more talk. "After we spoke on the phone last night, I checked my daughter's room. There's no box of pins and pens and what-ever else. There's nothing." Now the flat of her hand cut straight across the air. "Nothing. And you have to admit, it was such a *detailed* fib. In fact, it's what convinced me that our meeting today might be a good idea. I'm beginning to think that the girl, Amandine, is quite evidently disturbed."

I had dropped Amandine's dragonfly pin into her book bag just yesterday. I just knew she would try to use my cigar box against me. Now I had nothing to hide. I sat straighter in my chair.

"I've got nothing to hide," I said stoutly to Mr. Serra. "Amandine's the liar. She drew these gross pictures and she made up stories all the time. The fact is, she's delusional." I had picked out the word last night, as I lay sleepless in my bed.

Mr. Serra coughed. "Yes, well. Hmm. You see, Delia, we have an information problem now. Because according to what Amandine told her mother, and according to what her mother told me, you . . . also . . . like to make up stories."

That surprised me. "No," I insisted. "*She* made up stories. She was always making up—"

"And that you lived, a little bit, in your own world. That you liked to play make-believe games about students and, *ahem*, teachers . . ." Mr. Serra coughed again. Remembering Amandine's brutal imitation of him, I could feel unwanted laughter bubble up in my throat. Mr. Serra frowned at my smile. "Little games of an unpleasant nature."

"No, I didn't. I didn't. I didn't, that was *her*."

"Also, that you insisted you had . . ." Now he stared at a piece of paper in front of him. A paper filled with conversation scraps, I realized. A funnel of lies straight from Amandine to her mother to Mr. Serra. "That you had an older brother. She said you talked about him all the time, as if he were real. She said that you once became very agitated when she questioned this brother's identity."

I went cold. A sweat broke out on my

upper lip. My one stupid lonely lie. Amandine had thought she would catch me with the cigar box but instead she caught me—by accident—with Ethan.

Carefully, I looked at my mother, who stared straight ahead, although every thin bone in her neck became visible. She leaned toward Mr. Serra, and then sat back again with a sigh. When she spoke next, her voice was level as if she were talking to a client.

"I'm hopeful that my husband and I can resolve this terrible misunderstanding, Mr. Serra. My feeling is that the best we can do is to maintain a noble silence until this all quiets down. The nature of the friendship between the two girls seems beside the point. We've probably taken up too much of your time already."

"No, no! The friendship is the whole point. It is! Amandine played much worse games!" I was frantic, as the yoke of blame slipped back over my head. It was so unfair, all of it. "You can ask our other friend, our friend, Mary . . . I already talked to her. She said she'd tell . . ."

"Reverend Whitecomb called me to ask specifically, on behalf of his daughter, that she not get involved in this . . . situation," said Mr. Serra.

My mouth gaped open.

"Of course, I understand," said my mother. "It's an unpleasant business."

"Mom," I begged, "the older brother thing was just—"

"How could you do this to Dad and me?" Mom broke in, turning on me. "What is wrong with you, Delia?"

"It was one dumb story," I pleaded. I was close to tears. "What I made up and what Amandine did are two totally different things. And her thing is way, way worse."

My mother looked weary, but she didn't

want to say anything more in front of Mr. Serra. "I think we're finished here."

Mr. Serra nodded almost imperceptibly, then stood and opened his office door.

As we left, I saw him press a card into my mother's hand. "She's a very good doctor, specializes in adolescents, if you ever need to talk . . . about . . ."

My mother took the card and tucked it into her purse with a nod. I knew she was too embarrassed to speak another word.

"I'm sorry." Mary's voice was soft and floaty as a cobweb. I could hardly catch hold of it. In the background, I heard Jasper bouncing a basketball on the Whitecombs' kitchen floor. I pressed the phone closer to my ear.

"I don't need sorry," I told her. "I need help. If you could come with me to Mr. Serra's office and explain about that picture, for one, it would really mean a lot to me."

"I tore up that picture," she said.

"Or how Amandine made up all those skits and then got us to do them with her."

"Delia, *I* never did those stupid skits. Not really. Listen, Amandine's just a person who's lost hold of herself. Or maybe all those skit people *are* the real Amandine. In the end, it probably doesn't make a difference. All I know is she's messed up, and I don't want anything to do with her. Besides, how I can really help with whatever happened between, you know, between her and your dad . . ."

"*Nothing* happened. That's the point. It's a lie, the way she always—"

"Delia, my dad and Mr. Serra both decided we should let it all blow over, and that I should keep my distance in the meantime. You can understand that, right?"

"Right." I slammed down the phone. I wondered what more there was to lose.

My parents were in the den, talking intently. I stood in the doorway. I had interrupted too early. They looked up from where they were sitting, side by side on the love seat. Their hands were around their tea mugs and their shoes were kicked off. They did not appear to be in any mood for goodnight hugs, not that I was much in the mood to give them.

"Once, Mrs. Gogglio made me tea," I said. I looked around. The only other place to sit in the room was a high-backed armchair, and Mom's briefcase was opened on top of it.

"That's nice," said my father.

"It was good. Irish breakfast. She had this funny Popeye teapot she found in—"

"Delia, Mom and I are talking. Go ahead and watch television in the living room, if you want. Come visit us a little later."

"There's nothing on television," I said. I began to back toward the door anyway.

"Read, then. Your mother and I have things to say."

"Can I listen? It's not like I don't know what you're talking about."

My father made a gesture of impatience. I pushed ahead anyhow.

"I know I failed, I know that, okay? But are you going to hold it against me for the rest of my stupid life?"

My mother laughed, a sad sound. "It wasn't Dad's and my intention to give you a stupid life. Just as it wouldn't be our intention for you to use things that are private and personal to this family in order to play strange little games with your friends."

"I didn't mean anything by—"

"A miscarriage is common enough, Delia, especially during a first pregnancy. But it's private, it's personal to a family.

That is, it was, until you decide to . . . to hurt us with it. Then it becomes . . . something else."

"I wish I'd been a boy," I burst out. My voice was too shrill. "I wish I had been anyone, instead of me."

"Now you're just talking a lot of crazy talk," said Dad. "Go to bed, Delia, all right? It's been a long day." He himself, I noticed, looked flat-out exhausted.

"Come give me a good-night hug." Mom reached out. I went to her. "Oh, Delia," she said softly, her mouth at my ear as she pulled me close. "What are you missing? What do you ever need?"

"Nothing, I guess," I answered, straightening out of her hug. "I guess I've got everything, don't I?"

There was nothing they could say that would make us feel better.

I left, closing the door behind me.

* * *

It was a long time ago; I must have been in fifth grade, that evening when my mother told me the story of me. We were living in Connecticut at the time, and Lexi Neumann's mother had just given birth to twins, but one of them was sick.

"Remember the Neumanns in your prayers tonight," my mother said when she came to tuck me into bed.

"I don't know why everyone's so upset," I'd mentioned. "Whatever happens to the sick one, they still have a whole other brand-new baby."

My mother had leaned down and cupped my face in her hands. "A mother's love cannot be measured," she said. And that's when she explained how hard it had been to have me. She left out nothing, even telling me about her late miscarriage and the years of hoping that came afterward, and her story ended with the happy day I was born. The happiest day of her life, she said.

It was the miscarriage part, though, that seemed the most romantic and sad to me, the part of the story I locked onto. I asked my mother if she knew whether the baby would have been a boy or girl. A boy, she answered.

"But if that first baby had been a girl, then what would my name have been?"

"I don't know. I never had a second-favorite girl name," my mother answered, adding, "and I never had a second-favorite girl. You are our only one. Now good night, Delia."

I was glad to hear that, and so I don't know why exactly my imagination invented a secret brother, but from that night forward, he was always there. A big brother with my mother's grace and my father's charm. He became everything I wished I could be.

In real life, the sick twin got well, and Lexi had two loud and healthy little sisters living in her house. She always said I was luckier being an only child than an oldest, but none of her reasons convinced me. I think she was only trying to make me feel better.

Mrs. Gogglio clapped her hands when I agreed. The car almost swerved out of its lane.

"Wonderful!" she said, gripping the steering wheel again. "Now then, will you come in with me on Sunday to meet Melvin? He's the manager in charge of volunteering."

"What makes you think I'd make a good volunteer?" I asked. I felt reluctant, even unhappy that she had sprung this on me. What did I have in common with a bunch of old people? What did I know about taking care of them?

"You're a five-star listener, for one," she replied.

"But if I'm no good at it, Mrs. Gogglio, then I don't want to keep going."

"And I wouldn't press it on you. All I'm asking for is an honest try. You can give that, can't you?"

I nodded yes.

"If it works out, I'll readjust my own schedule so I work Sundays and take off Mondays. That means you'll ride the bus to school on Mondays. Think you can handle the bus, just for a day?"

I nodded again. "Really, though, why do you want me to do this so bad?"

"Because I think you'd have a talent for it," she answered firmly.

Spending my Sundays at Sunrise Assisted did not seem too thrilling, but it wasn't as if I had anything else to do. I think Mrs. Gogglio realized that, as well. The school week had become a stack of days to get through, and the weekend a tense anticipation of the next stack about to be served. At home, the strain and silence were almost unbearable.

By the next Sunday, I found myself being introduced to Melvin and touring the halls and grounds of Sunrise Assisted. In my regular blue jeans paired with an issued white smock and an identification badge—Delilah Blaine—I felt unfamiliar to myself.

"They need you," said Melvin, when I spoke up a few of my doubts. "It's a lonely business, getting old. People'll be glad enough that you showed up."

My first scheduled working Sunday, I felt like the new girl all over again, only here it didn't seem that I had much to prove. My duties were light and it was attitude, Mrs. Gogglio said, that was most important. At Sunrise Assisted, I had to be efficient and helpful, to put aside whatever was happening at school and home. As Delilah Blaine, I changed bedding, set up tables for lunches and games, collected stray golf and tennis balls, and held up the listening end on the slow unraveling spools of other people's lives.

In the beginning, I felt as if I was playing a role. In my baggy smock and false identification badge, I eased into my character, "Delilah," who was cheerful and unfazed. I learned how to deal with Mrs. Halliday, who was cranky in the morning, and Mr. Waters, who liked to sneak up to the roof. I understood how Ms. Gould liked her egg salad with chopped pickles, and that while Mrs. Lee loved outdoor walks, she also tired easily. I picked up some of Mrs. Gogglio's habits, too, the way she respectfully called her patients ma'am or mister, and some of her briskly friendly expressions. "Well, aren't you a sport!" Or, "Now who's giving me uphill on this lovely day?"

Eventually, I knew everyone's names and most of their histories.

"See? It's exactly like I said. You've got a real talent for people management, for caring and listening," said Mrs. Gogglio.

"Huh." I didn't believe her. I'd never had a talent for anything.

"It's true," she insisted. "People trust you with their stories, Delilah, and you're good at keeping the peace. It's a real nice part of your character."

That made me the exact opposite of Amandine, if my "talent," as Mrs. Gogglio called it, was actually part of my character. Amandine's talent was so different from her character that it seemed to pull her in an opposite direction. And I wondered if that was why Amandine didn't quite work as a whole person.

So maybe I was luckier than Amandine.

Maybe I got something that she didn't.

It was a weird thing to think about.

"You hardly talk to me anymore," I said to my mother, staring across the table at her one night during dinner. It had been nearly three weeks since the meeting with Mr. Serra. When I wasn't under Mrs. Gogglio's wing or sleepwalking through school, I was left to my own devices, to try to make peace and sense inside a house that seemed permanently shadowed by Amandine's lie.

"That's not true," she said.

"Or to Dad, either. You're so quiet all the time."

"I have a lot to think about, Delia." Now my mother clawed in her purse for her cell phone, which was rarely out of her reach. "I just remembered, I have to call work." She stood up. "If you'll excuse me, I'll only be a minute."

She disappeared into the den, and I looked down at my plate. I knew that even if I ate everything on it and went back for seconds, I would not get rid of my hunger. In this house, I would not get rid of the feeling of wanting more, not at dinner nor any other time.

That night, I woke to quiet voices. I slipped out of bed and crept halfway down the stairs. In the living room, I could hear my parents talking. I pulled my nightshirt over my cold knees and sat still, listening. In the past month, I had perfected the art of eavesdropping.

Their conversation was heavy with pauses, as if they had been at it awhile. Dad's voice was rough, thirsty-sounding. "Because we deserve to be happy, Eva. I can't drag myself through one more day."

"You have to stop—"

"Each day, the same. We've got to get away from here."

"There's nothing—"

"I walk into town and I imagine that a thousand pairs of eyes are staring at me. Accusing me."

A long pause. "Nobody's staring," my mother finally insisted. "A horrible little child, a child left alone with too much imagination. She's ill, she needs help. People recognize that."

For a moment, I thought that Mom was talking about me. My hand gripped the banister. The silence dragged.

"Such a strange, strange person for Delia to befriend," my father remarked at length.

"Oh, but Delia isn't the kind of girl who . . ."

But I had already raced on silent feet back up the stairs to my room. I couldn't bear to listen to the kind of girl I wasn't.

The power of one lie. It probably took a few seconds to tell, the amount of time it takes an earthquake to destroy a village. Now we were living in rubble.

Alone in my room, and again my anger had nowhere to go. I pushed back the covers and got out of bed, and tied myself firm into my robe. I made my feet heavy on the stairs, so that they knew I was coming.

My parents were tucked into shadows. Their faces reminded me of the pale, scared woodcut animals from Amandine's father's picket fence sculpture.

"If you want my opinion, I think we should leave Alford," I said. "I think we should go somewhere else. There's nothing for us here. There never was."

Then I turned around and marched upstairs. "*If* you want my opinion," I called down to them, "which I think you *should* want, by the way."

Summer had arrived. Green, soft, smelling

of tanning oil and grilled hot dogs. Lunchtime breezes rolled potato chip and straw wrappers like tumbleweeds across the lawn. I hadn't noticed spring, and that first perfect day took me by surprise. It was as if time had stopped for me somewhere in the middle of March, weeks frozen in chunks of gray ice. Now time had dissolved into a puddle behind me, and I was standing alone in the shadowless June sun.

I hardly saw Amandine. She had begun to hang out with a guy, Wyatt Roberts, a skinny sophomore who I thought I'd heard was in a band or had a brother in a band. Anyway, he was always wearing headphones and T-shirts of music groups, and soon enough Amandine had absorbed something of him into herself, and she began arriving at school wearing her own set of labeled shirts and rebel attitude.

Mary and I were friendly but not friends.

Friends were a luxury, I realized, and per-haps meant only for certain times in life. The job at Sunrise Assisted seemed to fit me best for now. In its own way, it gave me companionship, as well as a purpose and an identity. I was popular there, both with the residents and the staff. Popular for the first time in my life. One step at a time, Delilah Blaine was helping me come closer to the Delia Blaine I wanted to be, and I was learn-ing how to be friends with myself.

I had Mrs. Gogglio, too. Not only did she keep driving me to and from school, but our Sundays had evolved into a routine loop of work and lunch and maybe a little bit of shopping, afterward. When Odie MacKnight died, Mrs. Gogglio and I drove to his funeral, then went to a tag sale. I bought a letter opener for a dollar. The let-ter opener looked like something I might once have taken from someone else. These days, though, I didn't feel so much need to pull from what other people had. It was hard enough work to concentrate on myself.

Final exams came and went and then ninth grade was over, that journey finished forever. By then, my parents had put the house on the market and had a buyer.

"I hope you'll pick up the phone every now and again," said Mrs. Gogglio. We were sitting in patio chairs on her front porch, listening to the chimes clinking in the afternoon breeze. "Remember yourself to an old lady."

"You know I will. When I get my driver's license, I'll even come visit," I told her. "And I'll drive you around for a change. Only on account of *coincidence*, though."

She laughed. "I'll miss you, Delilah."

"Me too. But besides you, it wasn't that great here," I confessed. "To tell you the truth, I wasn't all that happy."

She flicked her hand through the air.

"Ah, nobody learns anything from being happy," she said.

I waited until the last week of school, when everything was passed in and packed up and over before I spoke again to Amandine. By then, I had assembled the things I most wanted to say.

She was sitting outside on one of the red-wood picnic benches that had been dragged out recently in honor of the weather and of the newly lazy senior class. She was wearing thick black sunglasses and a white dress thin as paper. Her body was too visible beneath it; I could even see the flower pattern on her underwear.

"Heard you're moving," she said brightly when she saw me approach. "Us, too. I'm so psyched. You know, this place is total backwater." She had a new voice; sleepy with a Californian slur on her *o* and *u*.

She sounded like Wyatt. Of course.

"I wanted to come by to tell you something," I said.

"Shoot."

I folded my arms over my chest and took a deep breath. "I wanted to tell you that I feel sorry for you, Amandine."

She bristled visibly, and made a show of looking me up and down. "That's a good one. *I* feel sorry for *you*, more like. You're like one of the total most boring people I ever met, you're not even smart at any—"

"Because, the thing is, you've got so much talent. You've got everything. You're an artist and an actress and a ballet dancer. You really are all those things. Those aren't lies." She shifted, listening. "But you never decided to use any of what's so great about you. And I was wondering why."

"Use. What do you mean, *use*?" she asked. Genuinely curious. She lifted her sunglasses and perched them on her head. Her eyebrows, usually penciled or feathered in the lines of this or that movie star, were plucked and bare. Her face looked bald, and I felt as if I were catching her backstage, the actress between acts.

"Like, why didn't you audition for the school play?" I asked. "Or do design for the school yearbook? Lots of times, you didn't even show up for art class. But you could have had your own exhibit or performed your own dance assembly. You're not shy. You'd have been amazing doing any of that stuff. You could have done anything."

She stared at me. Flat gray eyes that absorbed everything and leaked nothing.

"And what would be the point of that?" she asked.

"Well, so other people could *see*."

"But they do see," she corrected. "Other people are always watching me, Delia. I've always got an audience, no matter what I do."

She had given me an answer, sort of. It was the last thing Amandine ever said to me, and the only thing she ever said to me that might have been true.

In July, we moved to Boston.

We might even have gone back to the City, except that the Elroy-Bells had claimed it, although I heard that Amandine's parents had parted, officially, and had moved into different apartments in separate directions.

My parents are happy in Boston, and things are easier for all of us here, I think, because cities are good for groups. We are less a family than we are a threesome, venturing out to museums and dinners and plays. The city's impersonality and distractions create the right atmosphere for us to get along better, though. I think it has the right aesthetic.

I guess that has been some unexpected luck. Or at least, it's a start.

Amandine's apology arrived sometime in early September, before the beginning of the new school year. Handwritten for extra sincerity. It was a nice enough letter, but you could feel the other pairs of eyes—Roxanne's, and probably some concerned psychiatrist's—staring at the paper as Amandine copied the words neatly from her draft.

She had acted without thinking. She was ashamed. She was regretful. She was very, very sorry.

Well, that was what she wrote.

It did not sound like Amandine, this letter. It sounded like a character that she was playing. Even the handwriting was different, with little garnishes upward so that all her words seemed to be carried over choppy waves. I read it and reread it and discarded it. It made my parents feel better, though.

Even now when I think back on her, it is hard for me to put together a final judgment. I go back and forth. I pick up blame and put it down again. Perhaps none of it would have happened if I had not been as shy, or as eager, or as ready to believe in Amandine. Or if there really had been an Ethan, leading me in the right direction, soaking up some of the attention, releasing the pressure.

Then I wonder how much choice I'd ever really had, once Amandine turned her flat gray eyes on me, once she had me all picked out. And then I think that maybe I had no choice at all. Because if someone offers you a glimpse of their Ugliest Thing, what are the chances that you aren't going to look?